Signs of Life

Anna Raverat

Signs of Life

PICADOR

First published 2012 by Picador
an imprint of Pan Macmillan, a division of Macmillan Publishers Limited
Pan Macmillan, 20 New Wharf Road, London N1 9RR
Basingstoke and Oxford
Associated companies throughout the world
www.panmacmillan.com

ISBN 978-1-4472-1977-4 HB
ISBN 978-1-4472-0237-0 TPB

A CIP catalogue record for this book is available from the British Library.

Printed and bound by CPI Group (UK) Ltd, Croydon, CR0 4YY

Visit *www.picador.com* to read more about all our books
and to buy them. You will also find features, author interviews and
news of any author events, and you can sign up for e-newsletters
so that you're always first to hear about our new releases.

For Lola, and for Alfie, and for Vince.

It was a relief to know I had fallen
and could fall no further.

Sylvia Plath

One

Beginning this book, there is something you should know. This is not a confession. This is something I am writing; something I am making out of something that happened. Ten years ago I had an affair that ended badly. I have been trying to write about it ever since but I couldn't make it work and now I am beginning to understand why. I thought I had left the affair behind: there was a breakdown when it ended, a year or so of feeling numb, after that I got a new job, a new relationship that lasted a couple of years, later I moved house, gradually replaced all the clothes and shoes I wore during the affair so that one day I realized there was almost nothing left and I tried again to write it down. I suppose I thought there was enough distance, but it seemed I was still swimming in it, swimming against it, in fact.

A couple of days ago, I was reading a poem, and it wasn't the whole poem, just this bit of it, which broke the surface:

> how in time you do *not* move on:
> how there is no "other" side:

> how the instant is very wide and bright and we cannot
>
>   ever
>
> get away with it
>
>   *Jorie Graham*

When I read these lines I let out an involuntary *uh*, the sound of air being expelled by a low stab of recognition, a physical feeling in the belly, and I thought, *I am trying to get away with something*, and I sensed, for a moment, what I was trying to get away with, but it was so far back in my mind that it didn't have a shape, or not one I recognized as a thought or an idea. I wanted to haul it out and examine it and work out how to say it, but it moved quickly, like a small dark animal, and I only glimpsed its tail and haunches as it disappeared behind a ruined building. I panicked then, because I felt I had lost something terribly important, so I started searching and though I didn't find that creature, I began to unearth questions.

The first question was, what do I really know about what happened? Then a flood of questions and floating among them the awareness that I have not been honest enough and that was why I couldn't write well about it. Now I have to question what I think I know. I want to discover my part in it and take responsibility for that, if I can bear to.

What I have to work with are the questions, memories, and the notebooks. More scrapbooks than journals, my notebooks are like pockets for things I want to keep; in them I copy lines of poetry, verses from songs, descriptions of dreams, that kind of thing. During and after the affair, I wrote, haphazardly, about certain events and transcribed the worst things that were said in a hard-backed notebook with yellow covers and lined yellow paper that I took from work. Although the contents of this notebook evoke what I liked at the time, what I thought was significant, the descriptions of what actually happened are of limited use because they are so fragmented, either because I was writing code in case someone found and read it or because I was in a rush. I probably thought I would always be able to decipher the scant notes but after so many years I find that sometimes I cannot. And then there is what I remember and of this, though a few things remain, much is lost. Memory is not a pocket. It's like this. Here's the story: there are holes in it.

Two

This is how it started: I kissed Carl. I was working late and so was he. There were a few others dotted around the building, which was normal because most of the workforce was young and keen. At about nine he came over to my desk and asked if I wanted to go for a drink with him. We had only known each other a couple of months. I should have said no, because if I wasn't going to carry on working I should have gone home to Johnny, but I was tired of my work, he was persuasive and I was persuadable. I know that I intended to have only one drink and then come back to the office and finish up because although I took my bag with me, I left my computer on and papers all over my desk.

I had been dimly aware of Carl as a new person at work but the first time I noticed him was one afternoon in March when we happened to leave the office at the same time. I suppose he had been at work six weeks by then. It was unseasonably warm. We stood in the car park in the lazy glow of late afternoon sun, talking about holidays. The things that struck me were the stubble on his chin and the way he raised his head when he laughed.

Carl and I went to the bar just down the street. I liked this bar for its high ceilings and squat candles flickering in glasses on every table. No matter how busy the bar became, there was acres of room above everybody's heads, something luxurious about the unused space. I'm not sure whether the table hidden away in a nook in the wall was free when we arrived or whether we moved there after sitting somewhere else for a while. I don't remember how one drink turned to two, then more, or how he sat next to me on the bench we were sharing – was he turned to face me or sitting parallel? I don't know what we talked about, but I remember the quick energy of his face, his crooked smile and loud laugh. I remember that I drank a lot of red wine, but I don't remember what he drank. Neither Carl nor I had eaten any dinner, or at least I hadn't, and we didn't eat together. I smoked someone else's cigarettes, or bought some from the vending machine, something I did if Johnny wasn't around.

Somehow we got onto the subject of my sister's accident and the mood changed. I have a snapshot in my mind of how he was sitting just then, legs crossed, arms crossed in his lap, body inclined slightly towards me, eyes trained on me, mouth set in a way that lengthened his chin. His attention was a little unsettling, though I was grateful for his interest.

I remember this because it was a pivotal moment and because he was still new to me. Later I came to recognize that this was how he looked when he was concentrating.

My sister had been in a car crash a month before this night in the bar, and was badly hurt. There are only two of us, Emily is four and a half years older than me and we are close. I heard about the accident at work and Carl was there at the time, was kind to me, helped me get a taxi to the station. She's fine now (apart from a scar under her left eye) but at the time her accident was the worst thing that had happened in my life.

After asking how she was, Carl told me how sad I had looked as I left in the cab, and perhaps it was nice to hear that my outside had matched my inside. I was thinking about the loneliness of that taxi ride when Carl said, I wanted to give you a kiss; you looked so sad. I imagined him giving me a kiss on the cheek as I left in the taxi, the gesture of a closer friend than he was to me then. And then he said: Can I kiss you now?

Either because I was drunk at the time, or because it suits me, I don't remember what I said to Carl that made him go ahead and kiss me. Maybe it was a simple yes. And yet when he kissed me on the lips it was almost as big a surprise to me as when I found myself kissing him back.

A few days afterwards, I saw a woman in a supermarket who looked so much like me that I pulled up short to study her. She was weighing out oranges, carefully selecting each one. I stayed out of her sight, even though part of me wanted to march up and announce our similarity.

She was tall, with long dark hair, even features, oval face. It was only when she spoke to the man she was with and I saw the shape of her smile and her neat little teeth that I realized we weren't that similar after all. I checked my reflection in the metal panel surrounding the bananas. The surface was smudged, so my edges were blurred, but I registered that I was bigger than this woman – not just taller but heavier, curvier. We both had long dark hair, but hers was glossy and well cut and mine was pulled back in a scrappy bun, my face was wider and because it was the end of a long day there was mascara rubbed in under my eyes, my cheeks felt droopy and my lips were dry. I redid my hair, making the bun perkier, and applied lip balm. When I noticed that my mouth was fuller than hers, I felt pleased, as though I had scored a point in an invisible competition. She was still picking out her oranges – so slow! I walked past, throwing a backwards glance to see if she had noticed me. She hadn't.

Although that kiss with Carl was the first, I can see that it was not the start of our affair. Something must already have existed between us to enable that kiss to happen. I enjoyed Carl's company because he was irreverent and he made me laugh, but I didn't think I fancied him. He wasn't conventionally good looking; his nose was large and bent at the top where it had been broken once, and he was shorter than me – only slightly, but still.

I know other people had noticed his attraction to me because they teased him about me when I was nearby. Outwardly I ignored this while inside I was pleased with the attention. I was flattered, but refused to concede: it didn't suit me to have things that way round, and so I proceeded according to my version of reality in which Carl and I had a new and light friendship that other people couldn't quite work out. One day my assistant told me outright that Carl was obsessed with me. That's how he put it. Perhaps if he had phrased it differently I could have listened.

I loved Johnny. We'd been together five years, living together for one – no ruptures, no wrinkles, we were happy.

Johnny was gorgeous. Everybody said so. He was tall and broad, with the widest, most complete smile I have ever seen. Although youth and sport kept him trim, Johnny was prone to chubbiness; his good bone structure was always well covered. He had blond curly hair and brown eyes with thick lashes. Unusual, but he wasn't vain, which is not to say that he wasn't confident, he was, and sometimes arrogant but his arrogance wasn't about his looks. For instance, he refused to pay more than a few pounds for a haircut: the cheaper the better, as far as he was concerned. Once he found a place that scalped him for two pounds and came home looking like a coconut. The scrawny covering they left made his features seem oversized; normally I was proud of his plump, high cheeks and Adonis jawline but now he looked like a caricature of himself. I pleaded with him not to go back to that barber's shop but it didn't affect the sense of achievement he reaped from the cheap haircut.

To begin with, I was hardly ever alone with Carl. We worked in a busy office and any lunches or drinks were shared with other colleagues. But there was a trip for work we went on together. In the lead-up, we were conspiratorial; Carl kept buying things for our journey – music, sweets, cigarettes. I was happy to see jelly babies in the pile on his desk and he noticed and said: Could I please see that smile again? I loved that he said please. His courtesy was probably the thing about him I liked the most.

We left the office with a sense of triumph – we had escaped, and together. We snaked our way through the city and when we hit the motorway I drove really fast to scare him but he only cheered. The cigarettes tasted as good and as dry as biscuits. He played a CD of an obscure American band. The music reminded me of cold rooms. He asked me if I liked it and I had to admit that I didn't.

When we arrived in Leeds it was already dark. After driving around for a while, we found our hotel, went in together and discovered they had messed up our booking, had given us a double and didn't have anything else. Carl suggested we have a meal first, but I felt uneasy about not having anywhere to sleep so we got back into the car and drove on. At the next hotel, cheaper looking, Carl stayed in the car while I went inside.

The man at reception told me he didn't have any single rooms left, but he did have a twin and would that be all right? I would like to say that it was the hotelier's suggestion and the lateness that made me think it might be acceptable to share a room with Carl, but I admit that something inside me leapt at the chance. I remember this feeling as a kind of excitement. Perhaps it was an extension of the feeling I had when we drove away: that with Carl, life could take unforeseen turns. When I went out to tell him, I was elated. I had presumed it would be OK with him and it was. I see now that my behaviour on this occasion added up to an admission of attraction, but somehow, just then, I was convinced of my own innocence. At that time, I did not know how well I could lie. Once I knew what I was capable of, I stopped trusting myself and other people in quite the same style. Looking back, knowing I lied, I have to question everything.

A couple of weeks before the kiss, I felt it was time that Johnny and Carl met, and that I ought to meet Katie, Carl's girlfriend, so we arranged to see a band that Carl used to play with, he had been the drummer. It was strange, presenting my private self to my work colleague and seeing his non-work self, like showing each other part of our bodies. I liked Katie, or else I wanted to like her and wanting to like her was enough like truly liking her to pass as the same thing. She had bobbed hair, thin lips, a sharp little nose echoed by a sharp little chin and her eyes were made up with swoops of black liner. Overall, she seemed pointy. All evening I tried to measure how well Johnny and Carl were getting on and whether Katie warmed to me. Because I was watching the evening more than I was engaged in it, I felt on the outside of what was happening. I couldn't dance because I was too self-conscious, and when I saw Johnny dance in a ranging, roaming way I cringed as if he were doing something embarrassing. On the way home I asked Johnny what he thought of Carl, expecting that my new friend had made as good an impression on Johnny as he had done on me, but Johnny only said something like, He was OK, I suppose, a bit intense – the band was good though.

I found out later that Carl had already decided to pursue me and was only interested in meeting Johnny to size him up as a rival.

Is it possible to make something happen by wanting it enough? Can desire be that powerful?

Carl's first impression was that Johnny was 'a bit handsome'. Yet Johnny's handsomeness didn't put Carl off because Carl's mind was set. Desire alone is not, I think, enough to make something happen; you also need determination. I have experienced this in writing. Wanting to write is not enough. The trick, as P. G. Wodehouse said, is to apply the seat of the trousers to the seat of the chair. And to get the seat of the trousers onto that chair, day after day, and keep it there, requires desire, but also willpower. Desire and determination cannot guarantee the quality of the outcome, but they will get the thing written. Desire and determination were not enough to ensure a happy ending, but they got the affair started.

After the first kiss, Carl and I left the bar. The next bit I remember is walking through a housing estate not far from the office, a shortcut most of us used in daylight to get to the High Street. Probably we had decided to walk to the High Street to get taxis from there. We seemed to be in that housing estate for hours. There was talking, but I don't recall what it was about. Mostly, there was more kissing. Who are you? I kept asking him, but he couldn't answer me except with another kiss and each time that happened I asked him again, Who are you? Maybe I was asking myself that question. Maybe I meant, Who are you, that you can lead me astray like this?

He told me he'd fallen for me, hard. I brought up our partners and he brushed the mention aside as though they were no matter and should not be allowed to intrude. Still, I lingered and we held hands and walked slowly and kissed again and again. I was drunk enough to not watch myself, but not so drunk that the strangeness of the situation was entirely lost on me.

Looking back, even though those kisses were deliciously reckless, the best moment seems to have been before the first kiss in the bar, when an acknowledgement of the tension between us was surfacing but still unconfirmed, and before I had done anything wrong. I see now that since I stayed on in the bar with him after that first drink, and stayed there for a long time, drinking and talking and smoking, that what I was doing was prolonging that moment, and perhaps I was also waiting to see how the moment would culminate and where it would go.

When I got home from the bar, it was almost one in the morning and Johnny was beside himself. My phone was switched off so Johnny called the office after ten and got through to Ivan the workaholic who was the only one left by then. Ivan said he had seen me working not long before and since my computer was still on and my desk was covered with work, that probably I had gone to the loo or nipped out for something and I would be back soon. Luckily for me, Ivan had not seen me leave with Carl. Johnny asked Ivan to leave me a note to call home as soon as I got back to my desk, which of course I never did, so at eleven thirty Johnny got on his bike and came looking for me. He cycled round the streets near my office and by the time he arrived home it was well past midnight. I showed up just before he called the police.

I told Johnny that I had been in the pub with a crowd from work and that we had a lock-in and that I was sorry for being so inconsiderate. Incoherent, more like, he shouted. He could smell the booze and cigarettes on my breath and in my hair. We slept far apart in our king-sized bed, managing to avoid even brushing toes.

Three

I've always kept notebooks but sometimes I lapse, which is no good when there is something I want to get down and out. The other day, I opened the yellow notebook eagerly, trawling for information. I saw we went to see Carl's band on April 17th and today is 24th April (odd, that the dates nearly match) and the day after the band, I copied out lines from a poem, 'Elegy for a Drummer' (I loved that title, love it still), and this extract from the journal of one of my favourite artists (having bits of other people's diaries in mine reminds me of a picture by Escher of a hand drawing a hand, going round and round, in and in):

There are six ways to eat oranges
1) my father taught me to peel an orange in a spiral so that one could later put the peel back together to form an illusion-orange. can't blow bubbles or turn cartwheels so this was an important skill –

Now a days this always reminds me of the old irish custom from King Arthur where if one cuts a strip of skin all around the outline of a dead man and then lays it around a sleeping man then when he wakes he will love you. Of course if he wakes while you are laying the strip down he will die.

Francesca Woodman

Reading the quotes and extracts is like hearing old favourites come on the radio, things you can sing along to, but when I looked at what else I'd written I put it down quickly, bundled out of my flat in a hurry. I couldn't read the notebook, or not much of it, because as well as the unhelpful gaps, the me of ten years ago is intensely irritating to the me now – whimsical, self-absorbed and whiney like an annoying younger sister.

I ended up taking a long walk by the canal, the farthest along the towpath I have yet been (I may even have reached Limehouse). After an hour or so I was getting hungry and thirsty so I started back and it occurred to me that trying to get away from myself like this was a bit like running away from home when you don't really mean it.

And, I suppose, that although she makes me wince, I do still like the bits of other people's writing she wrote down.

Four

Where I live now is a one-bedroom flat in Islington. It's up three flights of stairs, which sounded too high and so I nearly didn't bother to see it, but my sister made me come and I liked it immediately. There is more daylight in the rooms compared to where Johnny and I lived in Hammersmith and I don't miss the garden because I never gardened. I like the little roof terrace I have here, which is reached by two French doors directly opposite my desk. What I can see through these doors is mainly the backs and roofs of other buildings. To my right is a tall church steeple with a weather vane that catches the light on low, pink evenings and the bells ring out at the weekend at seemingly random times (I assume the bells are rung by machine and I think the machine may be broken). There are three trees, but they are quite far away and not very tall and apart from the fact that they sway where nothing else does, they are unremarkable.

The building directly opposite is in a pitiful state. There is a tapas bar underneath that is well run and popular, but the two-storey flat on top has been forgotten. I haven't seen a light on. The black plastic drainpipe is broken and hanging down and flaps and bangs on windy nights and days and the wooden frames around the four windows are rotten and crumbling, the white paint weathered away. A sinewy buddleia has taken root out of one crack in the wall and looks feral, like a half-starved urban fox.

Today I am counting things I remember. I imagined this would be like opening a high cupboard and a whole load of stuff tumbling out that had been shoved in there and forgotten about for years. This hasn't happened yet.

I have counted the number of arguments with Carl and categorized them (mild, serious, vicious), and the number of times we had sex outdoors or in vehicles, and the number of times I avoided saying whether or not I loved him. (I didn't.) We kissed first in May but it was over by September, so the affair was short enough to count almost everything that happened in it. There was one birthday, mine. I turned twenty-four that summer, and something that seems curious to me now was that I thought of him as so much older than me because he was thirty.

We had one good-natured disagreement. It was about how many pistachios make the perfect mouthful. He said one at a time because then you keep wanting more. I said five, because the ratio of shelling-time to size-of-mouthful yielded more crunching, but then I am the kind of person who rips open a bag of pistachios, trawls through for the freebies – the ones that have come out of their shell by themselves – and gobbles them up. On one long car journey we experimented – I was shelling, he was driving – and agreed that fifteen was outrageous and ten too many, which made me doubt my position but I stayed with five because by then it had become one of those bonding jokes you get at the start of something, like knowing you can't win but wrestling anyway because you just want any and all physical contact because you know it will end in sex. This movement between play and passion was the best; I don't know exactly how it shifted, but suddenly the humour would give way to tenderness and then the tenderness would grow edgy, and it made the sex bigger, somehow. But when I think of those early, fresh days now (so few of them), it's not just sex that comes to mind, it's laughter. His laugh made a puppy out of me; it was something he threw out like a ball, hard to resist.

Almost all of my memories are fragments, impressions. For example, there was a conversation with Johnny about new work-friends – we were at home; I think it was a week-end. Johnny told me that he had made a new friend at work. What's his name? I asked, barely interested. Her name is Fiona, Johnny said. *Now* I was interested: Is she pretty?

Not really, he replied.

What does that mean?

It means you have nothing to worry about, he said. Then he asked: Do I?

Do you what?

Do I have anything to worry about?

I knew then, that he meant Carl, but I said: What do you mean?

Well you've got a new work-friend too, he said.

What, *Carl*? God, no!

Johnny relaxed into reading the paper again.

So now we both have new, non-pretty work-friends, I said.

Of the opposite sex, said Johnny. I never heard him mention 'Fiona' again.

I can't bear it that the start of the affair was also the beginning of the end with Johnny, mainly because of the position that leaves me in, but also because I don't believe things were that clear cut.

When I got home from being with Carl that first time I had to deal with Johnny and so it wasn't until he and I were lying far apart in bed that I began to think about what I had done and the thought was so hard and heavy that I turned quickly away from it and my drunken state helped me to turn off the scene so that I fell asleep without any trouble.

The first thing I noticed when I woke up was the cloying

sweetness of alcohol only a few hours old and a dullness like thick liquid that had seeped into every crevice inside my head. I began going about my morning: black coffee and toast, shower, drying my hair. Johnny barely spoke, still angry, which suited me because it meant I didn't have to tell the lie again. I knew he wasn't suspicious, because he didn't ask who I went to the pub with. I had never lied to him before.

Johnny and I did not argue much but I doubt there was genuinely less conflict between us than between other couples. If we wanted to be a couple who never fought, it was probably because we were so young when we met that we believed it was desirable, even possible, to be in harmony all the time. I remember one fight shortly after moving into the flat we bought together. We were having a break from decorating, sitting side by side drinking tea. An argument began, though I can't remember what about, and as it got more heated I shook my empty cup at him. Don't threaten me with a teacup, he said, and then laughed at how ridiculous that sounded. Most of our rows were resolved quickly and amicably like this.

On my way into work I tried to avoid thinking about what I had done, yet images of Carl and me in the bar and in the housing estate kept crowding forward. I knew that I would have to see and talk to Carl, but because I couldn't bear to admit that I had betrayed Johnny, I couldn't begin to prepare for that encounter. I had an image of the kind of life I would have with Johnny – a big house, a leafy lane. The details were slow and suburban, though I didn't see that then. I thought I could make my heart a private road: no speeding, no collisions, no thoroughfare, no heavy load. No entry.

I met Johnny on a research trip, along with thirty other students, in a tropical paradise off the coast of Malaysia. We met towards the end of the project, and his reputation preceded him so that when he arrived at the camp, I was wary of him and looking for faults – I decided that he wasn't as gorgeous as I had heard, nor as laid back. But after a few days he won me over and we got together by a fire on a beach in the moonlight. Our magical beginning was something we referred to as if it bestowed a certain grace upon us. But now that I think about it, there were problems. Yes, there were the sunsets over the ocean, the dolphins swimming just offshore, the fresh coconuts, the fishing boats sailing past – but Johnny had already had an affair that summer with a French girl, and it was camp gossip that they had been seen having sex on a beach. It was this that had hardened me against him to begin with. When the project ended and all the students regrouped, Johnny received a lot of attention from the other men about the French girl and I became jealous and rejected him. Whenever he and I looked back we saw our beginning as perfectly romantic and glossed over all of this. If I chose, even unconsciously, to remember the good and forget the difficult on this occasion then it makes me wonder how many other uncomfortable memories my mind has suppressed.

Ivan's note lay on top of the papers spread over my desk. He'd used thick black marker pen on a big piece of paper. The note said: Rachel, please call Johnny ASAP, Ivan. I scrumpled it up quickly and threw it in the bin. I didn't look up as I tidied my desk; scared that someone would meet my eyes and give me a look that would tell me they'd guessed it all.

After my sister's accident, the day I went back to work, I found a photograph in the top drawer of my desk. The picture was of the office manager, a man who took the limited powers his job gave him very seriously. People laughed at him behind his back. Carl had written 666 on the office manager's forehead. It made me smile. That same morning Johnny had had to leave early and when I was getting ready for work I found a note on the kitchen table. The note said: Cheer up. I didn't feel cheered, I felt I had received an instruction.

Carl and I went out together at lunchtime to a cafe I had never been to before and where we felt sure we'd find no one else from work. We sat opposite each other on burgundy banquettes that were smooth enough to slide on except for the patches of silver tape over cuts in the leather. Carl looked tired and though he listened, he already seemed to know what I would say. He didn't protest when I told him it had been a mistake and must never happen again. I got the impression he felt strongly for me and felt I was leaving him and that he was taking it hard, even though we had barely been together. I was worried that he would tell someone and asked him not to. I must have asked what happened when he got home, whether Katie had been angry that he was so late, but I can't remember his answer. The way Carl behaved made me think well of him and made him more attractive, though I couldn't admit this at the time.

One reason I wanted to let Carl down gently was because I already knew about his family. Carl's father died when Carl was six years old and his younger brother four years old. Their mother never recovered from the loss. She slid into a depression from which she never fully emerged and, after a few attempts, she killed herself when Carl was fourteen, his younger brother twelve. His younger brother, who I only ever heard Carl refer to as 'Our Kid', still lived in the house they had grown up in and where his mother died. It was in the outskirts of a city by the coast that I had never visited.

A dream I recorded in my notebook around this time: I am standing in front of a large white house on a grassy hill that slopes down to the top of a white cliff far above the sea. As if in a bowling alley, I am rolling balls of fire, one by one, down the slope and they drop off the cliff into the sea where they are instantly extinguished, steam hissing up from the surface. The mood of the dream was calm, I remember it as pleasant though puzzling – what was the fire that I was extinguishing so methodically? Occasionally I still dream about Carl, and also, though less often, about Johnny.

Carl chose all his clothes well. He knew what suited him and he didn't mind spending a lot of money, even though he didn't earn a great deal. I especially liked the way he looked in blue jeans and heavy boots, the way the denim, soft and pale in places, showed off his thighs, which were strong and well shaped, not too broad. He wore reddish brown workman's boots, shiny with age and wear.

He was attractive because he was confident and I think he was confident because he knew he was good at sex. After the awkwardness of the first few times, we soon became fluent. For him I learned to wear silk camisoles, tight cotton vests, to leave them on until he said, Take off your top – and then do this in one smooth motion. Although the way he watched made me feel like a goddess, his fierce regard induced in me a kind of disorientation – a sense of discovery that didn't lead anywhere; with him, I was never really sure whether I was more myself or less myself.

I was nervous about living high up but in fact I like it better than being on the ground floor. I fantasize about growing strawberries and lettuce on the roof terrace, though in reality I almost never go out there (I have my desk almost flat against the doors and so it's tricky to open them). But I am trying other new things, like wearing my hair down instead of always scrunched back and buying luscious shower cream instead of unscented blocks of soap and making tea in a pot with actual tea leaves. Living up here just suits me.

> It is very nice to have feet on the ground if you are a feet-on-the-ground person. I have nothing against feet-on-the-ground people at all. And it is very nice to have feet off the ground if you are a feet-off-the-ground person. I have nothing against feet-off-the-ground people. They are all aspects of the truth, or motes in the coloured rays that come from the coloured glass that stains the white radiance of eternity.
>
> *Stevie Smith*

Johnny and I went camping in Corsica. We found a perfect place to stay; a little patch of flat, mossy ground for the tent, a river, shade. The day after we arrived there, I sat by the river, reading. Johnny said he wanted to go for a walk and set off up the steep side of the valley. Whenever I looked up from my book, I could see him getting smaller as he climbed. Later he returned with a small yellow flower. He'd seen the flowers high on the hillside through binoculars and decided to go and pick one for me.

During that holiday, my birthday came around making me feel low, as birthdays sometimes do. That evening, as it grew dark, Johnny crawled into the tent carrying a fruitcake with candles on it, something he'd planned before we left England. I remember his face in the candlelight, especially his warm, wide smile.

Sometimes I would dearly love to see Johnny again, to talk with him, hear his sense of things. I don't even have his phone number.

If I couldn't make the kiss unhappen then I wanted it to have been a simple mistake, something that happened because I was drunk. But I had been drunk before, many times. I didn't have to decide whether or not to tell Johnny, I simply knew that I would not. Telling him would make the act bigger than it needed to be, and as I made myself see it, not telling Johnny the truth was an extension of the mistake, not a separate act, and so I had only done one wrong thing. One wrong thing in five years of a good relationship didn't seem so bad. If you took the mistake and divided it between all the days and nights we'd had together the mistake became so small that it almost disappeared.

Because of what happened later, I destroyed or threw away everything Carl had given me. When it turned nasty

I wrote down as exactly as I could, with dates and times, the threats he made to me in case I ever needed them to use as evidence against him. But when it was all over I tore these pages out of my notebook. Now I wish I hadn't. I am not a particularly well-ordered person, and I wonder whether well-ordered people have accurate recollections and people like me have to put up with a jumble. I can never be bothered to put my washing away – I just take what I need from the pile of clean laundry on a chair in my bedroom. This lack of order used to nag at me, and I would berate myself for not being a better person. Even though I now believe that order is over-rated, my doubt over what happened, and when, presents a problem in writing things down. Sometimes this doesn't seem to matter, but other times it does. For example, the conversation with Johnny about new work-friends: I can't remember when this took place so I can't tell whether Johnny was looking for reassurance early on, before anything had happened, or whether it was later. Although I have said I was sure Johnny was not suspicious the night of the kiss with Carl, the fact is I don't know for certain. I don't know very much at all about how it was for Johnny.

I do still have a photograph of Carl. It is at the bottom of a box of pictures that I have been meaning to put into albums for years. I remember taking out all the other photos

– the envelopes at the top were dusty because the box has no lid – and laying the picture against the brown cardboard at the bottom, piling everything back on top. I did this quite deliberately, as though I was hiding it from myself. The photograph is of a group of colleagues. We worked closely together for a time and there was a great sense of camaraderie between us, but I am not in touch with any of them now. In the photograph, Carl is crouching on the ground and smiling up at the camera, squinting slightly against the sun.

I don't know why I kept it. I thought I had washed my hands of the affair. Did I keep it as a souvenir of the darkness?

Yesterday, I went to the cupboard in the corner by my bed (awkward to open because the room is too small, really, for the bed, which I brought from the old place), found the box of old photos and took out the picture. Thick grey dust stuck to my fingers, I was surprised how soft the dust was, I thought that's how fog would feel, if you could touch it.

Johnny's best friend Juan would have been able to tell me how fog felt because he was a climatologist involved in milking clouds to obtain drinking water. The technology was basic: nets. I remember him talking about special atmospheric conditions that occur along the Pacific coast of Chile and southern Peru, where clouds settling on the Andean slopes produce dense *camanchacas* – perfect for milking. In the foggy season it is possible to collect enough water every day for a really big family. Juan was passionate about desert fog. His eyes lit up every time he mentioned the mists of Iquique in northern Chile, where he now lives, I believe, possibly with a really big family of his own, trekking through the Andes with a giant net, catching clouds.

The photograph was at the very bottom of the box, as I remembered, inside a plain brown envelope, which I don't remember. Finding it didn't solve or satisfy anything. I couldn't write afterwards. It has been an effort to write again today. There is something in the back of my mind, just out of sight, troubling me, something – like the photograph – I have kept but can't look at.

Five

The week after I told Carl it had been a mistake, he asked me to go to lunch with him. I had misgivings, but since we started out as friends and had agreed to continue that way, I went. He was quiet, almost shy, on this occasion. I still knew very little about him and I think he was aware of that and was being careful to show himself in the best light he could. He apologized for what had happened that night in the bar and this pleased me because it meant I didn't have to take any responsibility. He had bought me a bottle of expensive perfume and offered it to me tentatively, perhaps thinking I wouldn't accept it. The gift made me anxious straight away: there was Carl's gesture, there was Johnny's ignorance of the whole matter, there was my surprise at being given this perfume. I have since become much better at saying no, but back then I found it hard because I imagined I was disappointing people. I got myself into awkward situations where I said yes to an arrangement for the same time with more than one person and then had to try and combine the plans or back out of one. Since I was more confident letting down the people I knew well, I got into trouble with members of my family and old friends for messing them about. Until they got angry with me I didn't see what I was doing and then, although I knew they were right, I resented being told.

I accepted the perfume from Carl, even though it was not the wholesome thing to do. I guessed that Johnny wouldn't notice its appearance on the bathroom shelf, and that even if he did he would assume I had bought it for myself. Just as it didn't seem possible to refuse the gift, it never occurred to me that I could have taken the perfume and kept it at work, or given it to someone else, or thrown it away. I am not saying that these would have been good things to do, just that they were options that I didn't see at the time. Although I may have felt bad for Johnny's sake about taking the perfume home, I didn't examine the guilt and I didn't see how Carl was now in my house, on my skin, or how I had put Carl's feelings above Johnny.

Carl looked at me as if I were an international femme fatale. He didn't care who else noticed, in fact there was something defiant in him, something daring others to try and interrupt him.

One day, I arrived at work to find Carl's three team-mates around his desk discussing something in whispers. Carl himself was nowhere to be seen. I didn't want to seem too interested so I ignored the fuss and started work. A few minutes later the chief executive came up to our floor with a visiting dignitary. Carl's friends immediately formed a row along the front of Carl's desk. The chief executive and her guest stopped to talk to them and they remained standing in a row as if for some kind of military parade. Afterwards, Carl's friends were jubilant. They called us all over to have a look: Carl was curled up fast asleep under his desk and they had been hiding him with their legs. His friends loved these small acts of rebellion. And so did I. We worked in a charity dedicated to young people and we travelled around the country raising money, setting up events to instil leadership, determination, team-work, things like that. Many of these young people had had a tough time, seen and done things way beyond my experience – one told me that before stealing a really expensive car, he would steal a suit first, so that the police would be less likely to stop him as he drove around. I was impressed by his creativity. I got used to confiscating knives but was shocked once when I was cooking with a group and a girl asked, What's that fucking green thing? It was a courgette.

Although Carl liked the young people at least as much as I did, and had more in common with them, his job seemed to be of no importance to him. He started to care when I managed, after several attempts, to break up with him. By then he had lost me, long since lost Katie, was about to lose his flat, and so his job was all he had left. But he was so angry with me for leaving him that he couldn't help using work as a way of punishing me and he behaved so badly so often that he also lost his job.

Today, when I sat down to write, I noticed scaffolding on the flat opposite. Now that I work from home I look at it every day. It is in a late stage of disintegration. The grey metal framework looks like it is propping up the building, but maybe it is too far gone and they are here to demolish it.

There were three visits to the seaside with Carl. On the first, we walked along the promenade with a giant cloud of candyfloss. I remember soft pink wraiths coming away from the ball, turning granular in my mouth, feeling thirsty afterwards.

In the arcade he exchanged banknotes for heavy bags of coins that we used quickly. He won and was pleased. I lost every time. While we were eating chips from grease-spotted bags a seagull swooped low and crapped on my head. I yelled out in surprise – the worst thing about it was the warmth! I had a mouthful of hot vinegary chip, which I spat onto the promenade. Carl laughed, but then he went to the van where we had bought our chips and got a big pile of rough blue paper towels and pulled the shit out of my hair as best he could and picked up the greasy bag and spilled chips from the ground, even the one I spat out, and put them all in the bin and offered to buy me more. I didn't want any more. I noticed the two fat ladies in the chip van laughing into their hands and did then see the slapstick side of it. One of the ladies came out of the van and gave me a polystyrene cup of hot, bitter tea. She told me it was lucky to have a bird shit on your head and on the train back to the city when I was picking out dried stiff bits Carl reminded me of this and I objected: You won a tenner, I got shat on – how does that make me lucky?

Accepting the perfume was a mistake. It was allowing him in. It made the second time we kissed possible. If I had said no to the perfume, then maybe the first time would have been the only time and I could have cut it off and set it adrift.

On another holiday with Johnny we followed a path along a river one day. I remember luxurious heat, baked earth and a warm, sweet scent that I think was fig trees. I walked behind Johnny because the path was narrow. There was a quietness between us. I could see sweat breaking out on his back. His hips bulged slightly at the waistband of his shorts and the white flesh beneath the line of his suntan kept peeking out. I remember this picture of him because it was one of those moments when I was aware of loving him.

There were plenty of other people around, tourists and locals, sitting in the sun and in the shade, reading, talking, eating, and swimming in pools in the river. At one pool, a waterfall dropped about twenty-five feet into the water. A group of lanky boys were climbing up the rock to the right of the waterfall, jumping in, climbing up again. Johnny joined them. I watched him climb up and move out to the jumping ledge. Before he jumped, he retied the cord of his trunks, caught my eye and grinned, and then he dropped into the deep green water, and resurfaced within seconds, seemingly with the same smile. After watching him a few more times, I wanted a go. Johnny climbed up the rock behind me, coaching me on handholds and footholds, but there was only room for one on the jumping ledge. You go first, I said, thinking it would be easier to jump if he weren't just over my shoulder. Sure? OK, see you down there, and he made his way to the ledge and jumped off again, easy as anything. The younger, browner, thinner boys hung back, waiting for me to make my jump. I followed the route Johnny had taken to the ledge. The ledge was tiny, there wasn't even room to stand properly; you had to have both feet facing in the same direction, towards the waterfall, and lean into the cliff for support. The rock below swelled out like a belly: I would have to jump out quite far to miss it. Johnny was treading water in the pool, smiling up encouragement. He looked a lot further away than I expected.

No way was I going to jump. Cautiously, I made my way back from the ledge to where the queue was, scared and embarrassed. Johnny scrambled up to meet me.

What happened? Are you all right? It must have been

harder to get back from that ledge than it would have been to jump!

Maybe, I said. But you can't jump slowly.

A few months before my sister's accident, Johnny and I started arguing more and the arguments didn't die down as quickly as they used to. I went shopping with Delilah and bought a pair of designer shoes made of silver grey satin. They were beautiful, like frosted glass. The shoes had high heels and I knew they looked good because they made me feel fantastic. I had never worn shoes with high heels before because I was already tall, at school it was undesirable to be any taller, at university I spent all my time in trainers, so by the time I was in my early twenties I had no idea how to walk in heels and somehow thought I wasn't allowed to wear them. Delilah encouraged me to buy the shoes and I was grateful to her for opening that door. Johnny objected to the price I had paid and I resented this because it was my money. I wanted him to be bowled over by the new me in my glassy satin shoes and he wasn't, which robbed me of the elation I had come home with.

It bothered me that I wasn't brave enough to make that jump from the waterfall. I told Johnny I wanted to go back. The next morning the pool was in shade and the water looked as black and solid as tarmac. All I had to do was jump. But I couldn't make myself do it. I tried several times to gather up my courage into a jump but I simply couldn't do it. Something inside me had already made the choice to stay put and I couldn't override it.

Just let yourself fall, shouted Johnny.

Don't be stupid, I said, but he was right because once you are whistling through the air falling and jumping are the same thing.

It was easy for Johnny; he knew he could do it. His self-belief was so strong it was almost an aura. Now I see how he used it as padding between him and the world, but back then I thought he was wonderfully secure. Even when he danced badly to his African music, he did it with such conviction that it seemed fitting. Twice while we were driving on a motorway, Johnny thought he recognized people in other cars: There's my old maths teacher! he shouted, and waved at a car as it overtook, and, another time, I went to school with her! The first time I was impressed by the coincidence and tried to get a glimpse of his old maths teacher as the other car sped past, but the second time we quarrelled because I laughed. He insisted he was right and sulked until I conceded it was possible that he had again correctly identified an old school mate in high-speed traffic.

On a beach holiday with Delilah I brought one bikini and she brought four.

Four bikinis! We're only here for a week! I said. She laughed.

I thought you were only allowed one, I said, quietly dismayed as I realized I wasn't joking and that this was, in fact, what I believed.

No, said Delilah, kindly – you are allowed as many as you like. We went shopping and I bought two more, *and* a new pair of sandals, and I know it was only bikinis and shoes, but I really did feel the world had opened up a little.

But Johnny disapproved of Delilah, he thought her frivolous because she cared about clothes and liked parties and occasionally took drugs and, perhaps feeling this, Delilah was not impressed by Johnny, finding him judgemental. Johnny's bluster may have been covering unease, but he really did seem to think he had the right to disapprove and to have the last word, and I let him.

Our director organized a team-building day for the whole department. We all sat round in a circle in the briefing room on the top floor while a woman of mid-height with mid-brown hair made us introduce ourselves to each other as if we'd never met before. She lost half of us right there. When it came to her turn she said, I'm a lucky lady. I have a wonderful husband and twin girls, aged three, they're beautiful but a bit of a handful! We all laughed obligingly except Carl. She went on to describe the prize-winning village where she lived, her pets, and how she did team-building work because she loved helping people. Carl took the piss out of Lucky Lady all day long and although I felt sorry for her as she struggled to stay on top of his heckling mainly I was glad because her dreariness was choking.

That night I took Johnny to the pub. I wanted to tell him about Lucky Lady and I needed him to get it. I told him about the life she'd described and he thought it sounded attractive so I tried to explain the way she didn't understand that not everyone would want her kind of life: neat and tucked in, and how she put all her energy into shoring up her pocket of reality. But that's what everyone does, said Johnny, and I see now that he was right, but because the conversation wasn't going the way I wanted, and because of the mood I was in, I bummed a cigarette off someone and smoked it in front of him, and so we ended up arguing about that.

I suggested to Carl that we play Russian Roulette, with eggs. I hard-boiled eleven of the dozen, wiped off the water sediment and placed them back in the carton. I let Carl move the eggs around without me looking, but I made him do it quickly so he couldn't weigh or examine them. We played it with cards; when you lost a hand, you selected an egg and smashed it on your head. Carl got the raw egg, which evened out the seagull incident, though he took it better than I had.

I see how easily I recall moments when things were taut and full of promise, and forget much of what happened in between. For example, the perfume Carl gave me: I can still see the sparkly new bottle filled with clear amber and I remember placing it among the other bottles and tubes on the bathroom shelf, feeling a pang because Johnny had made that shelf and here I was polluting our home with scent from another man. But when half the perfume had gone and the bottle had gathered dust on its little glass shoulders, what then? Even if I had worn it every day I couldn't have finished it by the end of the affair because the affair didn't last that long. I know I didn't keep it, because I made a point of dumping everything Carl had given me, but I also don't remember throwing it away.

What am I supposed to save? What am I supposed to remember? What am I supposed to tell? Am I supposed to hold anything back?

The scaffolding has been up for days. I think the building will be coming down soon. I find myself wishing they would restore it, I am not sure why – I have no special attachment to this flat, I just happen to live opposite.

Six

Johnny and I were invited to a party in a new bar in Soho. I planned to wear the glass-satin shoes we'd argued about. Johnny didn't want to go to the party; I persuaded him by asking Juan to come too. The club was small with steps leading down to the dance floor where people were standing to talk. It was like an empty swimming pool. Soon the steps were jammed and everyone was dancing. I picked Juan because he was Johnny's best friend, and I thought his presence would help Johnny enjoy himself or at least give him someone to talk to other than me, but Johnny hated it. Juan danced very well. We danced. Johnny stood at the bar, looking down on everyone. After an hour or so, he wanted to leave. They're all posers, talking crap, he said. I looked around the room: They're just people having a good time. But Johnny was already in gear. He wanted us to go back with him to a pub near our flat and looked crestfallen when first I said I was staying, and then Juan said he would stay too. Johnny made his way to the door. I watched until I could no longer see his yellow curls bobbing above the sea of other heads.

Even though I was sad to see Johnny go, I enjoyed the

party more without him. That same weekend we had a row about fashion, although I can't remember whether this was caused by me staying at the party or something else. Johnny took the moral high ground: the shallowness, the sweatshops; I defended the right to care about how one looked and pointed out to him that he too followed fashion in his own small way, otherwise why didn't he dress entirely from charity shops? We ended up in the only two separate rooms in the flat. While I sat and pretended to work in the bedroom, I thought of a way to laugh it off whilst at the same time making a point. I unearthed some tatty old clothes, kept for the spring cleaning or gardening I never did, and dressed up in them. I tucked the top into the trousers and pulled them right up above my waist, like Tweedledum or Tweedledee. When I showed myself to him we did laugh and he took a photo of me.

Another time, we were walking in the countryside talking about some friends of Johnny's: this couple looked exactly like each other, same height, same build, same square face, same wide eyes, same fair straight hair. I thought this went beyond average levels of narcissism. But Johnny defended them: I think it's good when couples are alike, I think it helps them stay together.

Differences are good too, I said.

Yes, when they complement each other.

Well, then they're not really differences, are they?

—

Carl took some of us from work to the climbing wall he used. It was in a large echoey hall that had the same feel as a school gym. The wall was dark red with half-moons and other shapes screwed on in no discernible pattern and climbing at various heights were young men in black leggings with chalky hands and rubber slippers. Their bodies were lean and well proportioned, like Carl's, and they gave off a certain relaxed confidence, also like Carl. It was the first time I'd seen Carl as part of a group; he looked like them, he moved fluidly like them – he was in his element.

He gave me a lesson but I didn't like it much because I felt clumsy; I preferred to watch the way the best of them skimmed up effortlessly. When he saw I'd had enough, and that I was watching the others, he asked me to hold his T-shirt while he practised on the most difficult part of the wall. We were there as friends with others from work, this was before we had kissed, and he wasn't the only one to be bare chested, but when he took off his white T-shirt and gave it to me, it was a message. I watched as he scaled the wall, the way his body could stretch and reach. He was showing me his strength and agility and his lightness of touch.

When I complained to Juan about Johnny leaving the party, he told me:

He is a good man, it doesn't matter.

Yeah, I know, I said, thinking that it *did* matter, and that it mattered every time Johnny told me off for having a cigarette, or told me to turn the music down, or disapproved of the time and money I spent on clothes.

He loves you, said Juan.

I know, I said, feeling weary.

Later, Juan said something else to me about Johnny: If you *ever* leave this man, he began, and because of the way he started the sentence, with the emphasis on 'ever', I thought I was about to be told off, I thought he was going to say, you are crazy, or you are stupid, or something like that, but I was mistaken because what Juan actually said was: If you *ever* leave this man; give me a call. So now the emphasis on 'ever' sounded more like impatience or frustration on his part and changed the meaning of the whole sentence.

I have to admit that I liked Juan. But what had I done to make him think he could say this to me? Danced with him, smoked with him – I suppose that's enough. I didn't want to take Juan seriously so I decided that he was joking around and that it was probably more of a general appetite than a specific desire for me. Anyway, I never took it up. More than anything, it would have been unbearable for Johnny – not just my betrayal of him, but Juan's as well.

Johnny and I had one fight that gave rise to a moment that later seemed to be the end of a period of quarrelling and the beginning of our separation. Maybe this is the moment that I have been looking for, the one where our relationship ceased to be possible.

While we were fighting at home on a Saturday, some friends called round and instead of pretending that everything was fine, I told them we were in the middle of a row. I remember their discomfort and their efforts to be diplomatic. One of them suggested a game of cards and the other rolled a joint. They left soon after that, and Johnny and I resumed our fight. We began to argue about how we were arguing: he made statements as if he knew the world inside out and resisted my ideas; I remember feeling that what mattered was his refusal to admit my viewpoint too. I saw that when we laughed things off, it wasn't really making up; it was avoidance. We were scared to disagree perhaps because it went against the idea we had of ourselves as being harmoniously in love. I also believed, although this may not be true, that it was me who usually backed down and something inside me hardened into a refusal: this time let him be flexible, let's see if he can do it. He couldn't, or at least didn't, so I left.

Furious with Johnny, I went to Shirin's flat. It took forty minutes' hard walking to get there and I was even angrier when I arrived because all the way there I had been dredging up examples of Johnny's arrogance and what I thought were his other crimes against me. I explained things to Shirin, who was kind enough to listen closely. She liked Johnny but agreed he could be a bit moralistic. Later that night as I was lying on her sofa bed, I had a realization: *I have to leave him.* There was no emotion attached to the thought, it just came, unbidden, with the clarity of an instruction.

I stayed at Shirin's for three days. I wanted Johnny to sit up and take notice. And I was enjoying being with her. The bolt from the blue about leaving him scared me so much that I talked myself round: there's no need to leave him; I just need to do my own thing, like I used to. For example, once I went to China for three weeks. There was a reason why Johnny didn't come, though I don't remember it now. It was great travelling round on my own, if a little daunting, but this time I didn't want to go to China. Maybe I thought I could overlook what was wrong, maybe I didn't have the courage to face it, maybe I just didn't want the upheaval. In any case, I ignored the insight. All I have to do, I told myself, is see more of my friends, go out more without him, anything to lighten the constant clinch we hold on each other. This is where Carl and Johnny first overlapped: I had just started getting to know Carl and I allowed myself to believe that what I wanted was friendship.

Once, I was in a motorway cafe on my way back from a meeting in another city and I bumped into a man I knew through work. This man was a senior manager in a company we did a lot with and quite a bit older than us, so I didn't expect him to mess about, but while we were having a cup of tea he took out his phone and called Carl. Guess who I'm with right now? he asked Carl, winking at me.

Once we made pizza and the dough was too wet and sticky. I left Carl with a pair of gloopy white gloves, and went to the shop for more flour so that we could rescue the dough from his hands.

Another time, in a dodgy pub, he told me an intricate story about pirates that involved folding and tearing up the menu and at the end of the joke the menu was a little pirate T-shirt. I remember wrinkled peas with that meal, so over-cooked that they couldn't try and escape the fork by rolling away. Peas are supposed to be plump but these ones were shrinking away from their skin.

The fire door by my desk was open every day because of the warm weather. Carl would come and smoke on the fire escape. I started smoking more – having a cigarette gave us a reason to be together. Sometimes other people joined us, sometimes we climbed the metal staircase to the roof. Under the guise of staying friends, we found out more about each other and work provided endless opportunities for little chats, little lunches, little kisses. At first I didn't tell anyone what was going on and because it wasn't spoken about, it didn't seem real. One evening on my way home from work, I bumped into Delilah.

How are you? she asked.

I kissed someone from work, I said.

Oh!

More than once, I said.

Oh!

I'm not going to do it again, I said.

Right . . . Who was it?

This guy, Carl, we're kind of friends, but, well . . . And he has a girlfriend.

And are you going to tell Johnny?

No.

But do you still want to be with him? Johnny, I mean.

Yes, I said.

Well then I wouldn't tell him either, said Delilah.

If I had told my sister she would have put me right, but I didn't want that. I wanted to be able to have either one of them, or both of them, and for a while that is what I had. I wasn't seeing much of my family just then. At the time of my sister's car crash, and during the weeks of her recovery, I saw a great deal of her and my parents, and maybe that period was so intense that we all needed some time off from each other afterwards. Besides, a terrible thing had just happened to my sister's friend, and my sister was busy looking after her. The terrible thing was this: Her friend ended a long relationship because she'd met someone else and her boyfriend was so distraught that he hanged himself on a tree in front of her house.

The reason I kept stopping the affair was because I was going to marry Johnny. We weren't engaged; it was understood. Johnny proposed three months in. We were crossing a stone bridge on a foggy wet evening, a romantic setting but gothic weather. Halfway over he stopped to face me and took both my hands in his, holding me a little way off so that our arms made another bridge between us. The muffled light of a streetlamp was enough for me to see his face. He didn't look nervous, in fact he was beaming as though about to give me something I'd always wanted but he said my name a little too loudly and when he repeated it more quietly, it seemed as if the first time he was using my name to make a space to speak into, like someone clearing their throat, so perhaps he was nervous after all. After he said, Will you marry me? I made a happy sound and hugged him tight, but I didn't give him an answer. It was too soon. During the brief silence while I squeezed him, I wasn't feeling like all my dreams had come true, I was just hoping to stall him because I didn't know. I've always assumed he took my reaction as a yes because we never discussed it and he never seemed to have doubt, but maybe he didn't take it as a yes, maybe he always wondered what it meant but was too afraid to ask.

I haven't revisited this moment for a long time, and now that I have written it down I wonder whether the gap between Johnny and me, that I thought opened up around the time of the party and the glass slippers, was always there. I think we were each afraid of falling into the space between us, and being lost. I think we wanted to close the gap and so we worked hard at our intimacy with frequent visits, letters and daily phone calls even though we were at different universities, separated by hundreds of miles.

I suppose we must have grown more secure as time went by. Once, after we left university and were living together but long before I met Carl, we were driving through the streets in our little silver car when I asked Johnny if he would be able to forgive me if I had an affair. He thought about it for a minute, and then sighed and said, Probably, as if he regretted that this was his honest answer. Then he put the same question to me; would I be able to forgive him if he slept with someone else? No, I said, trying to see it and only being able to imagine murderous rage and intolerable pain. I know, sighed Johnny.

I was curious about Carl. He was outside my experience. He told me that he once had sex with a girlfriend and then her sister, in the same day. He didn't tell me, or I can't remember, whether the big sister knew about the little sister and vice versa. I was fascinated that he had had so many lovers because I had had so few. Apart from Katie, and the sisters, the one that stood out was a girl called Lorna with bright red hair. I could tell he had loved Lorna more than he ever loved Katie because the few times he spoke about Lorna it looked like it hurt him to remember. I asked why he and Lorna had split up if there was so much passion, and he said things between them were too extreme. They fought a lot. He told me she hit him a few times. I asked if he had ever hit her back and he said no, but once, during a particularly vicious fight he shinned up a Stop sign at the end of the street and battered it until the metal buckled. After he told me that, I had a good look at one of those signs to see if it was possible to dent the metal with bare fists, and I think it was, although he must have hurt himself. When Johnny left and Carl and I were together, he confirmed that yes; he had been completely in love with Lorna, but now he loved me more.

I don't remember what I ate, only what I didn't eat, like the bag of chips I dropped on the promenade, and the wrinkled pub peas.

After my sister told me what her friend's boyfriend had done, the image kept flickering in my mind. I could imagine the rope: old and scratchy, the colour of wet sand. I imagined him making the noose before he left home, testing it with his arm. I imagined him tying the rope to the tree outside her house, how it gripped the branches. It would not give. He could see, with a part of his mind that felt distant, that the rope would burn and cut his neck, but he knew, with the bigger part that was driving him, that this did not matter.

The image was there and I think it was a factor each time I broke it off with Carl. But it didn't work as a deterrent because each time, after a few days or a couple of weeks at most, it started up again.

The strands I remember are knotted so tightly together. I want to single out my part in it: single out Johnny's part: single out Carl's part: single it all out.

The softest moment of the whole brief affair had a soundtrack. It wasn't the first moment; we had kissed once, several days before. I had already told him it couldn't go on. Nobody else knew. We were sitting side by side on a long blue sofa at his friend's and the friend had gone out of the room, probably to fetch another bottle of wine, and a song came on with words that startled me with their aptitude. I lowered my head to hide from his sight, perhaps because I didn't want him to see the words of the song make an impact on me, which would have showed us both that I was thinking about him, or perhaps because I wanted to kiss him again and couldn't admit this, yet. My hair was covering the side of my face. I could feel all of his attention on me, not in a burning, oppressive way, which it later became, but more tentative, as if he were calling me, unsure of being answered, and he leant over and gently moved my hair. It wasn't a flick. The movement was too slow to call a flick, which would have been playful, possibly. It wasn't playful. His fingertips did not touch my face; I so wanted them to. This was a fat moment, full of yearning, on both sides, yet so small, maybe ten seconds in the course of a four-minute song.

Anyway. I have heavy hair and straight away it fell back and the friend came back into the room. It was useless. The song was by Nick Cave and the Bad Seeds, and although the lyrics were about love and longing, the bad seed was germinating, though I would not have been able to put words on or even around this.

> Do you sense how all the parts of a good picture are involved with each other, not just placed side by side?
> *John Baldessari*

It is hard to tell where one part ends and another begins, and even if you can tell, there may be an overlap, and the overlap may not be evenly balanced on both sides. For example, it seems that the affair and the breakup both became possible in that one flashcard moment: *I have to leave him.* I said I was scared by that moment, but it was also enlivening. It was a simple shift of focus: instead of looking in, at what I had with Johnny, I started to look out, and what I saw was Carl. I thought curiosity about Carl came first, and desire came much later, but of course you are only curious about things that already hold attraction for you. I wanted to see what he was like, to see how I was with him. Underneath all my protestations, then and now, I wanted him. It was probably that simple but I had to complicate matters in order to let myself go ahead and act on my desire.

I still tell myself that I didn't leave Johnny for Carl, even though I was with Carl as soon as I left Johnny. I tell myself this: leaving Johnny was *something I had to do anyway.* What a marvellous coincidence that there just happened to be another man I wanted! For a long time I believed that the affair with Carl only became a possibility after things had already started to go wrong with Johnny. This has been an excellent place to hide. I'm not saying it isn't true; it may form part of the truth but sometimes part of the truth is no better than a lie.

Seven

I entered each of his habits as if they were rooms I had never been in before, looking around to see whether I might make myself at home. I didn't like all of his habits, but to begin with it may have seemed to him that I did because I was exploring with a fascination that held off judgement, if only for a little while. I discovered a way to get him out of a sulk. Once, when things were not comfortable between us, Carl walked out of the cafe where we were having breakfast. I drank a second cup of black coffee to put off the moment I had to encounter him again. It was sunny outside in the street, a beautiful fresh morning, like today. The car felt airless but I couldn't coax him out. He sat in the driver's seat with his back to me, I stroked his head, combed his hair with my fingers. We stayed there like this for some time, two bored monkeys, until a strange closeness had grown up between us again.

I came home one evening, I don't know where from, and as I turned into our street I saw Johnny drive up the road away from me. I didn't know where he was going so I ran back to the main road and down to the next street where he would almost certainly come out. Sure enough the silver car appeared. I waved, but he did not pull over. He stopped at the junction with the main road. I saw then that he was leaving me because the car was piled high with his possessions. I went to the window, already wound down, and asked where he was going but he didn't want to say. He was unshaven, and the shadow made him look gaunt, unless he had lost weight during that time and I hadn't noticed. What shocked me most was that he had a bottle of beer in his hand and this was something that Johnny would never, ever do. He didn't want my concern; he swigged his beer and drove off, leaving me standing in the road.

This picture of Johnny is still clear in my mind because although he was distressed, it suited him. He looked guarded, as if his only protection was to get away from me. I wanted him more then, just as he was taking himself out of my reach, than I had in a long time. I had taken him for granted for so long that I had stopped seeing him. All the time I was carrying on with Carl I couldn't look at Johnny because I didn't want to see what I was doing to him. It took him leaving me like this, his things in the car, drinking and driving, without telling me where he was going, to wake me up to him again.

Something else has been bothering me about the young man who hanged himself outside his girlfriend's house. It's this: on some level, his death was to be her punishment for leaving him. And she took her punishment: I saw her, she wept and wailed, she lost weight, she couldn't sleep, she stopped work for a while. After some time, she began her recovery, and a few years later she married. I'm glad for her, I am, it's just that, from a distance at least, there was something formulaic about the whole thing.

Long before Johnny left, Carl and I were scheduled to go on a business trip together. We had already started and then stopped our affair several times. The trip had been planned for months and would have been tricky to get out of without our director asking questions I did not want to answer. We were to have a week in Wales, making presentations to new funders and meeting existing ones. The Friday before we left, I got Carl alone on the fire escape. Nothing's going to happen in Wales, I told him. OK, he said. I had already booked and confirmed reservations for separate rooms in each B&B or hotel.

On Sunday evening I drove to his flat to collect him, the first time I had been there. He and Katie lived on the fourth floor of an old red-brick building. The lift was broken and as I laboured up the last flight of stairs I thought how if I lived there I would climb those stairs every day and what brilliantly toned legs and bottom I would have. Carl opened the door in bare feet; he was still packing in the bedroom.

While Katie was making tea, I scanned their front room. There were several climbing magazines, a few dried-out plants in brown plastic pots, and a bicycle leaning against a wall. Evidence of Carl's life intrigued me, as though I was surprised to find that he existed outside his allotted space in my world. Until then, the times we had been together were dreamlike moments, blips that could be ignored, but seeing his home and his possessions made him much more real and I was relieved I'd ended the affair before it got out of hand.

Katie came back into the room followed by a large black cat. I looked at the cat padding along at her feet and noticed that Katie's toenails were painted cherry red and that her feet were soft and smooth. I was conscious of my own feet, dry and rough like Parmesan rind, but also aware that Carl was attracted to me despite this.

As we were leaving, Carl picked up the cat, Molly, and cuddled her while he gave Katie precise instructions on how to care for her. He spent ages saying goodbye to Molly, and this may have been wishful thinking, but it struck me that Carl seemed to prefer his cat to his girlfriend.

We were walking past Cardiff Castle after the first meeting of this Welsh trip and Carl said, Let's go in. We wandered around the Roman wall and battlement walk and the rooms open to the public. I admired the painted walls and ceilings, losing myself in the faded murals of courtiers, kings and queens. I was aware of him being around without feeling the pressure of having him next to me, looking at the same things. It was the first time I had been with Carl in such a relaxed way and the more we looked round the castle the more comfortable I felt with how things were between us: it seemed to me that we'd at last managed to move past the attraction to become friends. I'm short-sighted like this with weather too: if the sun is shining when I leave the house, I somehow think the sun will shine all day and I don't take an umbrella even if the forecast is rain.

The picture of Johnny leaving me remains clear in my memory not just because he reminded me of Heathcliff but also a sense I have that it was staged. I don't mean he set up the whole thing, I don't think he was waiting in the car, engine running, until I walked around the corner into our street before he drove away, because although he might have guessed I'd try and head him off at the next street, he couldn't have known it. His distress was genuine, and he really did leave me, at least for a few months. I think that he was probably at home, drinking beer, wondering whether I was with Carl, because I was late and he knew about Carl at that point, and getting angrier and angrier until he decided to just pack up and leave. And so he would have loaded the car quickly, which explains why he left things behind, and when he came to get into the car, he was halfway through another beer and because of adrenalin and the effect of the beer he'd already drunk, either he didn't notice the bottle in his hand or he thought, Fuck it. I don't think any of this was planned. The staged moment came when I was at the open window, trying to talk to him as he was waiting for a space in the traffic: it was the way he swigged the beer before pulling out onto the main road, as if to draw my attention to the dark brown bottle with its red and white label, as if he were saying, Look what you've done to me. I may be wrong, but this is how it seems.

There have been lots of times when I have acted a part too. I remember once making love with Johnny when I was no longer attracted to him – I thought that if I went through the motions then the wanting might come back, but it didn't; it was awkward and sad all the way through. I had accepted by then that my involvement with Carl was a wrong against Johnny, although I still hoped to get past that. What I didn't know was how acting out feelings for Johnny that I didn't feel any more was another kind of betrayal. Or maybe it was the same kind, but felt worse.

Johnny found a heart-shaped stone on a cold beach. It was smooth and flat and grey and fitted easily in the palm of his hand. He bored a hole at the top, threaded it onto a dark blue ribbon and gave it to me as a pendant. Although I saw the sweetness of his gesture, I only wore it once or twice, and that was to please him. It wasn't just that the pendant didn't match my idea of what looked good; it was also that I didn't want to hang a stone around my neck.

In the gift shop at Cardiff Castle, Carl bought a Welsh love spoon for Katie, and a teaspoon-sized one for Molly. I was encouraged, thinking that if Carl was comfortable buying gifts for Katie in front of me, then things were settled between us. I bought a postcard of the castle to send to Johnny but I didn't buy him a Welsh love spoon because I didn't like them, and in the end I didn't send the postcard because I thought it might give him the impression I was having too much fun for a business trip.

I was being careful about how Johnny saw this trip to Wales and now I remember why: it was because of one night when I showed him a jacket the same as Carl's in a shop window. At the mention of Carl's name Johnny withdrew, and stayed quiet for the rest of the walk home. I didn't ask him what was wrong, because I didn't want to hear it, but as we were getting ready for bed in our tiny bathroom, Johnny said: Is there anything you want to tell me? I was sitting on the loo taking off my make-up and he was about to brush his teeth and he stopped and asked me this question, looking at me hard, as if he wanted to search inside me and fish out the truth for himself. The tap was running but he didn't turn it off to save water, as he would normally, perhaps because it had taken all his energy to ask that question and now he was focusing all his attention on my answer and didn't notice the running tap. I was wiping my eye with a cotton wool pad and this allowed me to squint up at him without showing my whole face and fake a grimace that was meant to convey: What are you talking about? But Johnny waited, and the tap was pouring water into the sink and down the plughole, and still he waited until I couldn't stand the running water any longer and I stood up and turned off the tap and said, No! And then I said again, more quietly, more kindly, more convincingly, No.

A pattern developed to our days in Wales: we had a meeting in the morning, visited the local castle, drove on to the next meeting and then to the B&B. We shared the driving and in the car we talked; about work, my sister, his younger brother, his mum, we also talked a bit about Johnny and Katie, but never about us.

One of the castles we visited was a sprawling ruin of pale grey stone some distance from the nearest town. At first we thought we were the only ones there but then we came across a man in a green jacket and a woman in a red anorak sitting on segments of newspaper inside one of the castle walls, drinking something hot from a thermos flask. Although they looked up at us they didn't say hello and neither did we. Apart from this couple and a few black wire litterbins, there was no indication this was a tourist attraction. The other castles had entrance fees, gravel paths, roped-off areas and teashops, but this one was raw. It was like coming across a mountain after days of travel through tame pastures.

At one corner of the castle walls, near where the tea-drinkers were seated, stood a tower, about forty feet high, intact except for the roof. I walked towards it leaving Carl to do his own thing. There was a narrow doorway and no signs claiming danger or instructing not to touch, so I went into the tower and saw a stone staircase leading to a high window, about thirty feet up. The staircase must have been built for tourists because it looked solid and new, and I could see a wooden platform below the window, purpose-made to admire the view. At the top I looked out. It wasn't, actually, a great view because the window wasn't high enough to see over the tops of the trees to the countryside beyond.

I heard scraping first, then hard breathing and a few little grunts as if great effort was being made, and it occurred to me that perhaps the man in the green jacket and the woman in the red anorak were having sex below, but then a hand gripped the stone windowsill, the other hand came over, and Carl's head and shoulders appeared. He climbed the last little bit and swung himself in through the window onto the wooden platform. I remember the rising and falling of his chest and his blue T-shirt dark with sweat. He stood catching his breath, looking at me with intent. I felt dizzy for a second, as if I might fall, but the vertigo was not because of Carl's climb up the outside of the tower or because the platform was small and it seemed a long way down; this was a feeling I'd had before with him. There was a delicious thrill of danger in it, there was fear of falling, there was the desire to fall. But my fear of letting go was greater.

The flat opposite has been wrapped in plastic, completely covered in whitish opaque sheets like a dead body. I think they will demolish it soon. I hope it doesn't take long. I don't miss my old place but sometimes I forget where I am, imagine I am there again. By writing down what happened, telling even the most difficult parts that I have never told before, I am hoping to be released from the pressure of this story, hoping to shake it off or out of me, to stop it crowding my mind, pushing all the way to the front and all the way to the sides so that there is no space. Yesterday in a busy station I saw a man coming towards me who looked enough like Carl that I put my head down, spun around and walked away fast. When I was sure I would be out of his range, I turned, breathed, and looked for him in the flow of people. Then I remembered that the man could not have been Carl because Carl is dead.

Eight

Today is incredibly sunny and windy. A biggish tuft of dry moss is scooting about on the empty terrace. A full ten days have gone by since I last wrote anything. I am waiting for them to tear down the flat opposite – waiting is not an adequate distraction. I've been to the pool a couple of times to take my mind off it. Yesterday I swam behind a man doing very fast freestyle, his out-breath rushed back towards me like bubbles in champagne.

A scene from the aftermath of the affair, but before I was hospitalized: I am on the floor in the corner of my tiny kitchen with my back against the humming fridge, cramming dry cereal from the box straight into my mouth, each pale flake a crater from the moon, bubbled-up and blistered-looking, my mouth dry as it crunches the flakes and turns them into moon-dust which scrapes and scratches my throat as I shovel in more and more and Good! because I deserve it.

You can't tell everything at the same time. I tried but I couldn't make it work. I thought I had to tell everything to answer the questions. This is what the people in the hospital told me, and I believed them. I found it impossible. Everything mangled together: this was my sense of it. But they insisted, and I could see why.

One problem with telling the whole truth is that it takes such a long time. The 'whole' deadens the 'truth'. All the little side stories creep up and sneak in. Boring little facts crush the truth out of the story. The more I tried to tell everything, the more I seemed to get away from the quick of it. I felt this straight away, but I ignored my instinct.

And I think, but I don't know for sure, that the wordless back of the mind feeling is where truth lives. It's a push-you-pull-me zone (I know but I don't want to know) – way too spacious. I need to introduce boundaries so that I can start somewhere and finish somewhere else. There has to be some structure to pull me through the fog.

I met my next boyfriend at the hospital, on the roof, smoking. He was sitting on a breeze block with his back to me. I knew he was a doctor by his white coat, and I could tell from the side of his face that he was terribly handsome. I felt myself blush as I asked him for a cigarette and wished I was wearing something other than pyjamas. He stood up. He said: What are . . . How did *you* get up here? I tell him, he relaxes. He is taller than Johnny, much taller than Carl and he has dark, short hair. There is conspiracy between us already because we are where we shouldn't be, doing what we shouldn't do and we especially shouldn't be doing it because he is a doctor and I am a patient. We are on different sides. Despite this, or because of it, or both, he is attracted to me, I can tell by the way he looks at me a second longer than required, it's a reflex, he can't hide it, also he drops his shoulders just a little, opens his chest slightly.

Going out with this doctor was a bad idea for all sorts of reasons. He shouldn't have asked me and I shouldn't have said yes, but he did, I did, and there we are, or were. We saw each other for a couple of years. It didn't work, but that's another story. I say it was a bad idea, but actually the first six months were wonderful. I knew I was raiding my internal drug supply but the high got me over some of the worst bits and anyway, he was a doctor, he could get me more. And I don't want to sound cold, but here was a handsome man who wanted me and I wanted him and though it didn't last, and it wasn't love, we had our moments.

Because I haven't lived here long, each time I go out, to the pool, or the tube, or to walk along the canal, I am struck by how different North is to West. It's a whole new tone and texture.

The frenzy of sun and wind continued all day. The moss-ball blowing back and forth was getting on my nerves so I decided to remove it. To do this I had to drag my desk back from the doors and find the key. The black tarmac was hot under my feet, I expected the moss to be silky but it was brittle and crumbly. I dropped it off the side. The terrace feels much bigger when you are outside. In between here and the church I spied a small courtyard with lots of different sized containers, a round flowerbed in the middle, a white wisteria in flower (I wish I could smell it) and honeysuckle climbing the walls.

Nine

I'm not sure about all of the questions, but I know one of the answers: sex. There was one business trip, quite early on, where Carl and I ended up in bed together. We didn't, in fact, have sex but we were in bed together, and we may as well have done because afterwards it made no difference. It made no difference to the fact that we were now on a new level, one from which there was no turning back, and it made no difference to Johnny when I eventually told him – he was just as hurt and angry.

Carl orchestrated the whole thing. One morning, I kissed Johnny goodbye while he was in the bathroom, and stepped out of our front door to Carl, who was waiting for me right outside in the work car, engine running, music playing. There was a long drive and a full day of meetings or presentations, about which I remember nothing. Knowing that it was going to be too late and too far to travel back home, Carl had arranged for us to stay at the house of a friend of his, who I also knew vaguely through work. This friend had one spare room with a double bed in it, which I was to have. Carl was going to sleep on the sofa. We drank a great deal of red wine with this friend. Sometime after we all went to bed, Carl knocked on the door and said he was cold on the sofa and could he please just sleep in the bed. At least I think that's how it happened. We spent the night on separate sides of the bed, I slept; Carl slept. I woke early to find him very close to me, I was lying on my back and he was on his side, I could feel his breath, his arm and erection touching me. He was still asleep. I want to blame Carl, I do blame him, but of course it was not all his fault. On this May morning for example, in the bed in his friend's house, it was me that woke him with a kiss.

I didn't want to leave Carl after we'd spent this night together: I felt close to him and the sexual tension was cranked up high. And so I didn't see Johnny until evening. He'd been expecting me home for lunch. He knew I'd been on a business trip with Carl, and he must have been suspicious when I said I'd be back late. Johnny and I were going to a party and he wasn't pleased when I called to say I would meet him there. He tried to read me when we reunited, I didn't want to look at him, didn't want him to see my face. The party was dark, loud and crowded, which gave me some cover but the feeling that there was something wrong spiked every exchange, coded every movement. It was as though we'd gone for dinner at our favourite restaurant and found the white tablecloth spread over the candlestick and glasses, wine bottle and water jug, transforming the familiar into a miniature mountain range, and we were sitting at this table, refusing to acknowledge the strange landscape between us.

Alongside my attraction to Carl, there was my love for Johnny. But my love for Johnny was dying because I was putting all my attention into Carl and the only energy I spared Johnny was to hold him at bay.

The first time I had sex with Carl, Johnny had left me only the night before. I last saw him in the silver car, drinking his beer and driving away. I was shocked to see him go and spent a miserable night, but I was also a little relieved; at least we didn't have to keep pretending. The next day Carl and I had another long drive (sometimes I think none of this would have happened if it hadn't been for work taking us all over the country). It was decided to stay somewhere en route, to avoid the morning rush hour and reach our destination on time. The real reason was that we intended to spend the night together.

The town where Carl and I went also happened to be the town in which my grandmother lived. The streets were so familiar. I had been going to Peterborough three or four times a year for my whole life. My sister and I call it Peter-boring. My grandmother was eighty-eight and her philosophy about presents was this: if I can't read it, eat it or put it in the bath, I don't want it. So we would take fruit and cake and biscuits and eat together on her big squashy sofa. I was close to her and it was strange being in that town and not going to visit her.

The hotel was on a long narrow road near the train station. There were several hotels along the road; I can't remember how we chose this one. Asking for a double felt unnatural. There was none of the secret elation of the time we'd shared a hotel room before. The whole journey had been awkward. I couldn't stop comparing Carl to Johnny: the way Carl gripped the steering wheel with one hand at the top of the wheel, where Johnny held it loosely with both hands at the bottom; the way Carl avoided making eye contact with me as he walked back to the car after paying for petrol, where Johnny would have smiled in through the window. Because of this constant comparing, Johnny was more present on this journey than the other times I had been with Carl when I had shut Johnny out of my mind.

The hotel room was small. Along one wall was a fitted wardrobe with mirrored sliding doors and you had to squeeze around the end of the bed to get into the bathroom, which had a shower but no bath. The mirrored doors were probably intended to make the room look bigger but since all they reflected was the bed, it seemed as though the room was taken up entirely by this looming bed with its pale pink cover.

I didn't want to be with Carl. I didn't want to touch him. When we walked from the hotel to a Chinese restaurant I left a gap big enough for another person to walk between us but that other person had left me and I didn't think he was coming back. All my desire had evaporated, and yet I knew that I was going to do it anyway. Sex was the destination our affair had been leading to and now, with Johnny gone, there was no reason not to. Carl showered before bed, and when I showered after him, it felt like a ritual.

It happened in the middle of the night. Carl said, Look at us, and gestured to the mirrored doors where I saw us, naked, having sex. Here I am with you, said Carl, pausing to savour the moment. I was already self-conscious and now I had to watch. I don't like remembering this, and although I have successfully forgotten many details of that first time, such as how he initiated it, whether I thought about Johnny, what we said to each other afterwards, how easily I managed to get back to sleep, I am left with this picture of me and Carl having sex in that vast pink bed.

I didn't fall in love with Johnny: I jumped. I said I was wary of him when we met because of the other girl he'd been with that summer, and that was true, but I was also wary because he was so good looking, so popular, and because the place was so romantic. I didn't trust all this and so I held back, watching, waiting, until a few months later when Johnny was staying with me. We'd been to the cinema on a mid-week afternoon. Afterwards we walked through a park and sat on a bench, watching people scurry home as the evening came down. The feeling between us was like warm blue water, very wide and very deep. I suppose that neither one of us wanted to break that feeling because we stayed as it grew dark. I remember Johnny smiling at me: his mouth twitched slightly, as though hewas so happy he just kept pouring into that smile and it became so full that it overflowed into these twitches at the corners of his mouth. How good it felt to be the subject of such a smile. The rush of people thinned out. Through the middle of the park was a path with streetlamps spaced at regular intervals. The streetlamps had come on without our noticing. A cyclist rode along the path and there was a rhythm to how the rider moved through the darkness, dipped into the light, moved through the darkness and dipped into the light. Johnny was already in love with me, and I could see that it would be all right to love him too. It was as though I didn't really have a choice because I *knew* it was right, but maybe I knew because somewhere inside I'd already chosen. Despite this, I hesitated: I was afraid, but I also knew that if I wanted to meet him there, I had to jump.

One evening, when they pinned me down, I explained my dilemma to Shirin and Delilah: Johnny is the perfect man for me, but it's not the perfect time, and therefore how can he be the perfect man? It wasn't a proper question, but I wanted an answer.

Delilah said: Johnny is not the perfect man.

Shirin said: You're too hooked on perfect.

Both of them knew, now, about Carl and though they never met him or even saw him, they didn't think he was the perfect man either. In fact, everything I said about Carl disturbed them. They didn't like the sound of Carl, they didn't like the situation I had put myself in and they didn't like what I was doing to Johnny.

Shirin said: I'm worried about you, you should stop it with this guy or else what's going to happen?

Delilah said: You should tell Johnny. Or stop. But you should probably tell him now anyway, it's gone that far.

But it was clear that I wasn't going to stop and that I wasn't going to tell. Delilah and Shirin told me later that after this talk they were even more concerned. They didn't know what else to do so they called in the big guns – they told my sister.

Something else made the first sex with Carl awful, although it didn't happen until two days afterwards. Other colleagues were attending the event we were driving to, including three friends of Carl who knew about our affair. We arrived late at the hotel and Carl's friends had already gone; we wouldn't see them until the next day. Carl pinned a note to the door of their room. He didn't fold the note or put it in an envelope, so I read it. At the end, he wrote, 'P.S. The Good Life.' When I asked, he said this was just a joke with the lads.

The next day I had breakfast with these work mates while Carl stayed in bed. One of Carl's friends alluded to the fact that Carl and I had finally had sex. I was surprised he knew because Carl hadn't seen his friends since we arrived. It turned out that Carl's P.S. was code and they all knew what it meant.

I returned immediately to our room to tackle Carl. I was angry at his laddish trumpeting, angry that he'd speculated and discussed it with them all beforehand, and angry with myself for getting mixed up with this idiot. I told him it was over between us. He cried and begged me to forgive him. I remember him sitting in bed, propped up by lots of pillows like an old lady, his lank hair and red eyes, and wanting to kick him. Hard.

Ten

The flat opposite is to be saved after all: the plastic sheeting has been taken down, most of the scaffolding is gone, and the place is swarming with builders. I don't mind all the noise and activity because they are signs of life and anyway, I am prone to daydreaming and the sudden bangs bring me back with a jolt.

Every choice involves a loss. By following Carl, I lost Johnny. Or I gave him up. I knew about choices such as which assistant to hire, which car to buy, whether or not to ignore the comments of builders shouted from the scaffolding (not the builders opposite; they are part of the 'Considerate Builders Scheme', there's a sign up that says so) – these were decisions made at the top of the head. What I didn't acknowledge was that some choices are made at other levels and it can take the conscious mind a while to catch on. Like when I tried to jump from the waterfall: the top of my head was saying I could but my feet had already said no. I don't know whether my body made the choice or whether the choice was made deep in my mind and my body simply informed me of it.

After Carl's 'Good Life' note, I didn't want to travel back with him and I certainly didn't want to be alone with him. There were three vanloads of people leaving that event in convoy. I made sure Carl was in a different van to me. An hour or so into the journey, Carl's van – he was driving – made an unscheduled stop. Seeing him pull off at a garage, I felt abandoned, which took me by surprise. Twenty minutes later, someone in my van said: Look, here they are! Carl's van came up very fast behind us and overtook. I was annoyed; yet more foolish antics, but also slightly relieved that he was back. I was sitting in the front passenger seat and I noticed that up ahead, Carl was dropping one white flower after another from the van window making a trail of flowers on the road that our van gobbled up. This went on for a few minutes. Everyone in the vehicle had something to say about it, but I knew this was his apology – or rather, because I was so pissed off, the beginning of one. On a long straight stretch of dual-carriageway, Carl slowed his van to parallel ours so that he was alongside me, with only a metre of fast moving tarmac between us. Carl held out the last white flower. Take it! Take it! yelled everyone in my van. I rolled my window down and took the flower.

—

I didn't want to let go of my first feelings for him, I wanted to stay inside the crush, and I suppose I didn't want to deal with my life; the job I had grown bored of, the flat that I couldn't quite afford and now, with Johnny gone, learning to be on my own. Even before the affair, when Johnny and I were fighting a lot, Carl was where my mind went. The disenchantment with Carl was only a couple of days old. There had been several months of feeding the fantasy and the habit of thinking about Carl and wanting him was still there and, I found, easy enough to resurrect. It's not like I hadn't seen the warning signs. I ignored them because I liked what he gave me. I thought I could dabble. It was like the beginning of an addiction, to kryptonite.

The intensity with which Carl looked at me took me by surprise at first. Once I even looked over my shoulder to see if there was another, more glamorous, woman; I didn't believe he could mean *me*, and this wasn't because I didn't think I was attractive, but rather that there was a wide gap between the kind of attention Carl paid me and me as I saw myself in my workaday life.

In a dream, I am at the top of a tall tower with a group of other people. The group leader, who is on the ground, yells up and a young man climbs over the railings at the top of the tower and jumps. He is in the air for a long time. The jump becomes a fall – his body tips forward, his head goes back, his knees bend up behind him – it looks like he is about to start spinning. He manages to right himself just before landing heavily on his feet. His legs buckle beneath him and he staggers away on the hard earth. Now it is my turn. I climb over the railings and I'm in a perfect position to let go, but I am terrified. I don't have a good handhold or a good foothold. I take off one of my hands to try and get more stable and that makes me even more precarious. I don't want to do it. The railings are tall and there's nowhere to put my feet. I struggle back over onto the solid tower.

I said I remembered Johnny's twitchy smile as we were sitting in the park but now I realize I could be wrong about that. I couldn't have seen his smile in the dark, so perhaps he gave me that smile on another occasion. Or maybe the memory of this smile is a composite of all the other times he smiled at me like that, and not attached to any particular time or place, in which case it's not really a memory but a floating image. I also say I loved Johnny and yet I treated him so badly, while still claiming to love him, that I have to wonder whether I did love him at the point at which I started with Carl or whether my love had disappeared, like street-lamps fading into daylight and switching off without anyone noticing.

—

I still have all the letters and cards Johnny sent me, though I've never re-read them, and I thought I'd also saved the heart-shaped stone pendant, but it turns out I was wrong. The only other thing I kept was his records, and that was an accident: when he left, he picked up the wrong box and took my records instead of his. We intended to exchange the records but that never happened, and now I still have his long after we lost touch. I never listened to them, partly because I stopped playing records, and partly because they are his. Once I took out the box intending to drop it off at the charity shop and ended up looking through the records. They were like postcards from Johnny's life, showing where he'd been and what he liked – up-beat African and South American bands, blues, independent labels, classical music I never heard him play. I took most of them to the charity shop in a carrier bag but selected a few to put back into the box and then returned the box to its place in the cupboard. I don't know why I'm keeping them. I wonder if he still has mine.

Eleven

For my birthday, Carl gave me a coffee pot, cup and saucer each decorated with a Man Ray image of a milky-skinned, long-limbed woman. Even though we'd just split up, Johnny sent me a book by an author I liked. Inside the front cover, wrapped in white tissue, were some pressed flowers: a buttercup, a daisy, a sprig of cow parsley and a pink campion. The cow parsley had dropped its tiny white petals leaving a green skeleton and the gold had drained from the buttercup so that it was more like a ghost of a buttercup. I loved the inexpert way Johnny had carried out his sweet idea. I was comforted by his tenderness but mainly his gift made me sad because it showed me what I'd lost, or thrown away.

On the evening of my birthday, Carl and I sat in my garden drinking cool white wine; it was another hot night in a long line of hot nights. We could hear the clatter from a nearby restaurant and at one point the whole crowd sang 'Happy Birthday'. Listen, said Carl, they're singing for you!

I smiled, but I remember feeling lonely. Homesick, even though I was at home.

Carl and I visited a grand country house. We'd been driving on the motorway and needed a break. Carl looked on the map and suggested this detour: there was bound to be a tea room, it wasn't far and it would make a change from motorway services. As we drove down the gravel road, a sand coloured mansion came into view. You should live somewhere like this, Carl said.

At the entrance a stout man in a brown uniform refused to let us in because it was closing time. Carl asked if we could whiz round: No. Could we at least get a cup of tea in the cafe? Look in the shop? No. The man got down from his tall stool and drew back the iron bolts holding the huge wooden doors open. He closed one side. Carl stepped over the threshold asking for ten minutes. The man refused politely. There was a brief, uncomfortable silence. Carl was standing in a gentle dip in the flagstones and I remember wondering how many centuries of footsteps it takes to wear away stone. The man started to close the second door. Carl came out of the house without complaint but I could see that he was frustrated. The doors were shut against us, the man inside. When I turned to go back to the car, Carl erupted: he shouted and beat the doors with his fist. I watched, feeling entirely separate from this red-faced, spitting creature. His anger spent, he followed me back to the car, rubbing his knuckles. I *wanted* to take you there, he bleated.

He went to smoke a cigarette in the tree-lined car park. I watched a blackbird dart from a tall green tree. I could tell by the way Carl drew the smoke into his mouth in hard fast pulls that he was still agitated. The blackbird flew back to her nest. How good to be a bird, or lighter than a bird – a small cloud, or thistledown, borne away on a breeze, no choices to make, no business with others, no obligations other than floating. It was a regal tree, with smooth grey bark, elegant branches reaching up into a clear sky.

> It's like being in a cloud that never rains,
> The way they rise above the storm, and sleep
> So bird-white in the sky, like day-old
> Infant roses, little unambitious roads,
> Islands not defecting, wanting to be rescued.
> *Medbh McGuckian*

The blackbird appeared again. Carl finished his cigarette, and crushed the filter into the gravel with the toe of his boot. I had no interest in him at all. Maybe he sensed this because he wandered away, head down, fists in pockets. I looked for the highest leaf on the tree, a habit of mine since childhood, but the wind was moving the uppermost branches, so I couldn't find it.

—

One night last week, my sister stayed over, unplanned, and after showering the next morning, she went to find some clean underwear to borrow. It was such a bright morning – impossible not to be cheerful about the day ahead and the possibility of a whole summer of days like this. I was making coffee when I heard her scream. I met her dashing, naked, from my room.

Fucking arseholes!

What?

Fucking *ARSE*-holes!

What?

Go and draw the curtains!

Ah: bonanza for the builders. I went to draw the curtains, as instructed, and in the flat opposite was a window-full of builders, grinning and waving. I couldn't blame them. I waved back.

Fucking cunts, she said, with a towel wrapped around her even though she was nowhere near the window now and the curtains were shut anyway.

Wankers, more like, I said, but she was too pissed off to hear the joke.

They *cheered*. And *clapped*, she said.

Well, they are on the 'Considerate Builders Scheme', I said and then, to placate, added: And anyway, who wouldn't cheer, seeing *you* naked? (My sister is very beautiful. We have a system of acknowledging this.)

—

Because we worked with groups of young people in isolated locations, it was company policy for all managers to do a wilderness medical training course called 'Far From Help'. I was away when everyone else did it so I had to catch up. The course was a long, long way away from London but the thought of an overnight train to the north of Scotland and three days and nights alone appealed to me and so did the name of the place: the Forest of Maibie.

This happened earlier, when Carl and I were on and then off, on again, off again, on again, and I knew I had to break that cycle, and also that I had to decide what to do about Johnny. I needed to decide whether or not to tell Johnny, and if I did tell him whether I was going to try and stay with him, if he still wanted me, or whether by telling him I would also be breaking up with him. I needed to consider whether the whole affair with Carl was just a painfully long-winded way of breaking up with Johnny.

The course was in a log cabin down a long track in the middle of the forest, accommodation in adjacent cabins. I remember nothing about the other people on the course and I don't remember much of what I learnt, though I passed the test, but I do remember the session on the recovery position: me turning inert bodies over and bending limbs into the correct pose, other people turning my inert body over, bending my limbs into the correct pose.

—

I went to see Johnny where he was now living. He had a room in a friend's house in a town an hour away. The house depressed me as soon as I saw it. Actually, the street depressed me first; it was a wide, curved street and so far from anything with any zest to it that the place felt dead. The house was pebble-dashed and the bay window had a mini roof of red tiles. There was nothing to see out of this huge window except other ugly houses. It horrified me, but I see why Johnny might have shored up in such a place, to hide and heal.

So I have sailed the seas and come . . .
To B . . .

a small town fastened to a field in Indiana. Twice there have been twelve hundred people here to answer to the census. The town is outstandingly neat and shady, and always puts its best side to the highway. On one lawn there's even a wood or plastic iron deer.

You can reach us by crossing a creek. In the spring the lawns are green, the forsythia is singing, and even the railroad that guts the town has straight bright rails which hum when the train is coming, and the train itself has a welcome horning sound.

Down the back streets the asphalt crumbles into gravel. There's Westbrook's, with the geraniums, Horsefall's, Mott's. The sidewalk shatters. Gravel dust rises like breath behind the wagons. And I am in retirement from love.

William H. Gass

Johnny's friend Robbie was ironing a shirt in the sitting room, watching television at the same time. I had got to know Robbie and his girlfriend while I was with Johnny; we had been on weekends to the country. I was sure that Robbie must be angry with me because of what I had done to Johnny and I was relieved that the TV was on because it gave him something to look at so that if he snubbed me it wouldn't be so awkward, but Robbie looked up from his ironing, and greeted me in a friendly way, and I was grateful for that.

Robbie and his girlfriend were sporty, and their house was littered with bikes, helmets, paddles, waterproofs, walking boots. There was a canoe propped on its side in the hall. I had been in that canoe on one of our weekends away, borne down the river, enjoying the motion until the canoe tipped over and I fell in. Momentarily I was trapped underneath in the water. I kicked myself free and came to the surface, cold but exhilarated.

Johnny's room was small and decorated with faded yellow wallpaper. The door was flimsy, made of something like wood but without its weight. Boxes of Robbie's papers were stacked against one wall and I remember feeling cross that they hadn't cleared the room for him. Johnny's stuff was piled against the other wall. He couldn't have needed his toolbox, his tent or his records while he was staying with Robbie. I didn't know at that point that the records in the box were mine and that his records were still in the flat. He could have kept everything there, but I suppose he didn't want to leave his things around me. Maybe he wanted to remove himself completely, be separate with his place and things elsewhere. But now his place was a small yellow room stuffed with useless things that belonged to him and still more useless things that didn't belong to him and I felt I had buried him there.

Soon after we bought our flat, Johnny brought home a large wooden 'R' for Rachel, painted gold. Some months later I saw a large golden 'J' and bought it for him. We stuck the two gold initials, the 'R' followed by the 'J', above the doors to the garden where they stayed for years, gathering dust. One day, the 'R' fell down. I found it while Johnny was out. The wood had split, but not in two; I picked it up off the floor, climbed on a chair and stuck it back in place above the door. You couldn't see the crack unless you knew it was there.

Every morning before the medical training began and every afternoon when the teaching ended I would walk in the Forest of Maibie (that such a place exists!) questioning what to do. It was not a beautiful place. There was no bird-song. The trees were dense, so not enough daylight came through to the forest floor, and the paths were not very wide, more like animal tracks, so there was this feeling of being closed in. I thought I should pick a course of action and follow it, but I was stuck. The secret of the affair could not be contained for much longer, in fact I suspected that Johnny had already guessed. Despite this, I couldn't formulate a plan about how or when to tell him. Maybe I thought that if I did nothing the problem would somehow disappear, and I didn't want to face Johnny's hurt and fury. I paused every now and then to look up but I couldn't get far enough away from any of the trees to gain a clear view. The thin trees towered into the sky and then bent in towards each other and the tops wove themselves into a mesh of leaves and branches. The forest seemed to be holding me, and not in a sheltering way.

Carl and I crossed the line at work many times and would have been summarily dismissed had any of the bosses found out. Once, we were entrusted with thousands of pounds in cash to set up a staff development weekend – we were supposed to buy food and drink, pay for accommodation and certain team-building activities such as orienteering and pot-holing. The event was to take place deep in the countryside. We drove to the nearest big town and spent the night so we would have the whole next day to prepare. Carl brought a deck of cards and we played poker on the floor of our hotel room – I remember wonderful stacks of cash – and drank whiskey from the bottle, until Carl said, What we need now is some drugs, and he took some of the cash and went out into the night. He returned with a small amount of cocaine and a lump of hash, and we stayed up most of the night playing cards, doing lines with rolled-up fifties, smoking joints. The next day I forged a receipt for the amount he had spent on the drugs. After this, we often shared a joint while driving back from meetings in work vehicles, and sometimes we stopped the car somewhere quiet. I would like to say I felt guilty, making such use of company resources, but I was excited by our bad behaviour, and at the prospect of getting away with it.

Once, before the first kiss, Carl wore a green shirt to work that I admired. It was a new shirt and he was pleased when I noticed. A couple of days later, he presented it to me, washed and pressed, and after some protest I took it home and showed Johnny, who barely raised his eyes from the paper.

As teenagers, my sister and I made up a game called 'Am I prettier than?' There were two answers: 'Yes' or 'Same As'. (There were only a handful of exceptions, where the answer 'No' was allowed. I suppose we had to have some 'No's to give the game gravitas, to make us feel it was serious, and it was serious. Even when played lightly.) We started with girls at school, going from average to the prettiest and most popular, and branched out to girls we didn't know (Am I prettier than Victoria? Nicola? Natasha? Yes, Yes and Yes. Am I prettier than the girl who works in the bakery? Yes) and then to famous people and icons (Am I prettier than that newsreader? Yes. That actress? Same As. Am I prettier than Princess Diana?). As I remember, we would play for hours, but that can't be right because it's quick to get through even twenty other women. Maybe it was an ongoing conversation that we kept picking up over a number of years, which is why it feels like we played it for so long. The only taboo, never broken, was to ask: Am I prettier than . . . you?

Since they struck gold here once, the builders have developed more of an interest in my window. This past week, there has been a lot of looking (but no waving, from either side). I can see them clearly; they are only about twenty metres away – if I threw something, they could catch it; if I shouted, they would hear me. I have to admit I am tempted to walk naked in front of my window as my sister did, just to see if I get the same reaction. Right now, there are four builders looking at me, one from each of the four windows. One of them is leaning out of the window, smoking. One of them is holding a mug, empty, I think, by the way he is tilting it. One, with a fat face, has a phone to his head but he is not talking, maybe he is listening or maybe he is on hold or maybe he is waiting for someone to answer his call. One of them is just standing, doing nothing except look at me. He is the youngest and the one I like best. I would choose him, if I had to. Each of the four men is unaware that the other three are also looking at me. The fat-faced builder holding the phone begins to speak. He turns away from the window. The spell is broken.

Maybe because Carl was older, maybe because he was new to me, I felt he knew something I didn't, a secret that I wanted to know too. Now I don't think it was as defined or as sealed as a secret, it was more open-ended, to do with how he approached life as an experience where finding yourself and losing yourself is the same thing.

I said 'spell' but it was not magical nor even particularly charged, this moment with the four builders; no intent at all, or not that I could feel – and I think you can feel these things. It was absent-minded, idling. They were on a break and I was something, a woman, to look at, or on, or through. Or was I four women?

I returned from the Forest of Maibie to the city by train and Johnny was there to meet me in our car. I let him fasten his seat belt but before he could start the ignition I started telling him about Carl. Small dark words flew out of my mouth like bats. As soon as they hit daylight they darted away for cover, but I knew he heard them because his whole stature altered; he bowed his head slightly and rounded his shoulders, closing in on himself. He kicked the floor below the dashboard very hard, once. Then he started asking questions. He looked out of the windscreen, over the large car park, to the buildings and bridges beyond, and asked his questions. How long has it been going on? When did it start? How many times? Where? Who else knows? What did you do with him? Did you touch his cock? Johnny didn't ask what I felt about Carl. He didn't ask what I felt about him. I saw that Johnny was assessing the damage, and that not having had sex with Carl was irrelevant to Johnny because the line, for him, lay somewhere else, and I had crossed it.

Twelve

Johnny didn't leave as soon as I told him about Carl. He drove us home. He asked me to choose. I chose him. He marched me to a phone box to call Carl and tell him it was over. I didn't ask why we had to go to a phone box, but I think it was because Johnny didn't want so much as Carl's voice in his home. He stood guard outside the phone box as I made the call, which was short. The phone call didn't change anything; there was no sense of relief, Johnny's mood didn't lighten. That evening there was a wide and empty silence like a canyon between us. Words had to be launched into it, and mine were so puny that most didn't make it to the other side. I made an omelette but although we sat down at the table, we didn't eat and after a few minutes Johnny got up and went into the bedroom. Eating had become an act too intimate to perform together. When I cleared the meal away, the omelette slid off the plates and landed with a surprisingly heavy thud at the bottom of the bin. Johnny came back into the kitchen and stood in front of me holding a Stanley knife in one hand, and a wire hanger with the shirt that Carl had given me in the other. He sliced through the shirt without hysteria, until it was a banner of green ribbons. The only noise was the sound of fabric ripping and shirt buttons pinging onto the floorboards and rolling away.

In high summer, when Johnny had gone to live in Robbie's house and Carl was staying with me almost all the time, there was a street festival near my flat. Carl suggested going but I said no. I didn't want to bump into anyone I knew while I was with Carl; I didn't have the energy to explain him. Instead we spent most of the weekend inside. For something to do, I washed and treated his hair. Because I used my own shampoo and conditioner his hair smelt like mine and I found that off-putting. I loaned him a dressing gown, wrapped his hair in a towel and he lay down in the middle of my bed so that I could massage his face. I remember studying him as he lay there: his closed eyelids were straight, like hyphens, and the lashes sparse. As I smoothed cream across his eyelids I felt his eyeballs move like quail's eggs under the surface of his skin. I wasn't used to seeing him so relaxed. Without the usual tension binding him together he looked older. No one's ever been so nice to me before, he said afterwards and I had a twinge of guilt because I hadn't felt as tender towards him as I had acted by giving him the massage. It was one of the few times we were close physically without being sexual, and I have to admit I didn't like it much. It made me uncomfortable when Carl said no one had ever been so nice to him before; there was something in the way he said it that made me sure he meant it, and in that instant, I saw that he was someone who had not been loved enough, that he wanted me to fill those caverns, and that I wasn't going to because I didn't love him enough either.

After this weekend, I was at home alone one evening and I found a strand of Carl's hair on my pillow. At first I thought it was one of mine because it was a similar colour, but something stopped me before I brushed it off the pillow and when I examined it, I saw it was a paler brown than my hair. I picked up this single hair between my thumb and forefinger and carried it from the bedroom to the bathroom where I dropped it out of the window.

The night I told Johnny about Carl was awful. Somehow we got through the evening, the uneaten omelette, the knifing of the green shirt, and went to bed. In the middle of the night I woke up, realizing first that I was cold because the cover had gone, and second that Johnny wasn't there. There were muffled sounds coming from the kitchen, but no lights on. I walked quietly across the floorboards avoiding the ones that creaked. The duvet was bundled up in a big ball in the corner and underneath it was Johnny, crouched on the floor, quietly sobbing. I knelt down and crawled under the cover where he allowed me to stay in the quilted darkness and hold him and whisper, I'm sorry, I'm sorryI'msorryI'msorry, until the words stopped making sense.

Carl and I were walking down a street on the way back to my flat after an evening out. He suggested meeting the following night and I told him I had already arranged to go out with some friends. He was quiet for a minute and then asked why I hadn't invited him. I said I didn't think of it. He demanded to know why. He said he wanted to meet my friends; he wanted my friends to like him; he wanted to be in my life properly. He was tight with anger. Lashing out, he punched the wing mirror of the nearest parked car. The mirror sprang back and there was a smash as the glass shattered on the pavement. We walked the rest of the way in silence. When we got back to the flat he apologized. I stroked his bruised hand, told him that I liked being with him, but even as I said the words, I felt myself shrinking.

Soon after, Carl went to Switzerland to go climbing. He was gone five days. It was a great holiday: I went clothes shopping, had a haircut, bought lovely new books. I drank wine at lunchtime and read and smoked in bed. Apart from the phone calls, from Carl and from Johnny, I enjoyed myself.

—

I visited Johnny at Robbie's house. We were getting on quite well that evening, a little shy in each other's company perhaps, but not too strained. We had a meal, and a drink, and then he drove me to catch my train. But something changed as we got closer to the station, and when he pulled over to let me out, he started to cry. He didn't turn away from me but he didn't want me to comfort him this time, and he didn't try to stop. He sat forward in the driver's seat, with his elbows resting on the steering wheel, his face hidden in his hands, his shoulders shaking, and cried. I sat in the passenger seat, witnessing his hurt, knowing I'd inflicted the wound. It was awful to see him like that. But even as I watched him cry, self-pity crept up and smothered my sympathy. I had my own sadness but I still found room to envy his; at least he was innocent; his pain was pure. My pain was twisted around guilt.

When Carl returned from Switzerland he was full of the snowy peaks, the mountain meadows, the heights they'd scaled, the sun he'd caught. The thing that seemed to have made the greatest impression on him was his friend's home, with his wife and children in a chalet in the Alps. Carl described the kitchen: white walls, big windows, stone work-surfaces lined with jars of coffee beans, homemade pickles and jams, bowls of fruit, bottles of wine, and always a big round loaf of the most delicious white bread; soft and moist, dense but not doughy. They ate this bread every day; toasted for breakfast, with slices of ham and cheese and tomatoes and lettuce for lunch out in the mountains, with soup and red wine in the evening; there was always enough. More than anything else in the house, this bread seemed to hold the magic for Carl; all the enchantment of someone else's life concentrated into the loaf.

Once, Carl and I were driving back from a meeting out of town and I told him to pull over. Why? he asked. Just pull over, I said. We got out of the car and climbed over a fence into some scrubby parkland where we found a clump of bushes and we crawled underneath the prickly branches to a space not even big enough to kneel up in, and had sex. I feel embarrassed recounting this now, but this is what it was like between us – greedy sex, with terrible table manners.

Other times, I felt repulsed by him. For example, at night, his snoring would wake me. When Johnny snored, I would poke him and whisper, You're snoring, and he would mumble, Sorry, turn onto his side and I would snuggle up to his warm back and we would both continue sleeping as if uninterrupted. It was different with Carl, not because his snoring was so much worse, but because I hated to wake up and find Carl instead of finding Johnny. I wanted to punish Carl for not being Johnny, because I still thought I should be with Johnny even though I had broken Johnny's heart and pushed him away. I didn't want to poke Carl because I didn't want to hear him grunt as he turned over, or worse, have him wake up. And so I would sit up on the pillow, listen to his loud curly breathing, like a pig's tail, and look at him lying there in my bed.

Johnny and I decided to carry on but a few days later he packed up and left. For ages I believed Johnny had changed his mind, or that he had mistaken his mind in the first place so that having thought he could handle my betrayal and, in time, move on from it, he found after a few days that he could not, or would not, and so he packed his things into the car and left. But then I ran into Robbie in a bar and we were drunk enough to talk about Johnny. Robbie said that just after Johnny had decided to try and work it out with me, I stayed out late again with Carl. Being sneaky came easily. If I had bothered to look, I would scarcely have recognized myself next to the person I was before. Qualities emerged that had not yet fully developed: I was selfish and narcissistic, cold and mean. I didn't like being this way, but I continued behaving badly. It was shocking how far I was able to deceive myself: while I was a liar and a cheat to Johnny I was busy being Carl's perfect woman. In fact it was by lying and cheating that I made space to be that other woman. At the time I didn't see the contradiction, or if I did, I didn't care. I was quietly thrilled by my ability to be cruel and I wanted to be somebody's femme fatale, maybe it didn't matter whose.

The first attempts at writing this story sank partly because I had mistaken my project in the first place. I was wrong when I thought my project was to answer the questions by telling the truth, the whole truth, and nothing but the truth, because the very notion of the whole truth is a myth, and I was wrong again when I switched to trying to tell the truth as objectively as possible, because the idea of objectivity is another myth. The whole truth, the objective truth: such attractive ideas. I couldn't get inside using these routes. Someone else may have been able to, but not me.

The second visit to the coast, when we stayed the weekend in Carl's mother's house, we went out for a drink on Saturday night to get away from Our Kid. The streets were full of people, some in couples like us but mainly in single-sex groups of four or five, and although there was a sharp wind coming in from the sea, I remember seeing a lot of bare legs and bare arms. We drank something in one bar and moved on to the next. I drank red wine, served in very large glasses, and noticed that nobody else was drinking this although lots of other women were drinking white wine out of the same very large glasses. Like most of the other men,

Carl drank pints. I smoked more than usual, which means I chain-smoked. I was bored. I wonder if he felt bored too. We had been together constantly for three days at this point and although, later, I was often bored when I was with him, unless we were eating or drinking or having sex, this was the first time I was aware of it.

I recall thinking that the cigarettes I was smoking, not my usual brand, were the only visible point of contact between me and the people here. I displayed the packet like a badge or VIP pass. It lay on the table and every time I reached out to flick open the lid or picked it up to pull out another cigarette, I noticed that the same blue and white packet could be seen in dozens of other hands, poking out of shirt and jeans pockets, in handbags, imagined it on tables in pubs and bars across this large and unfamiliar town, to which I would never gain, nor want, really, membership, and so on me, this packet was a form of fake ID.

And each time, without fail, Carl would light my cigarette with a lighter he kept in his front jeans pocket. He was smoking too, though not as much as me, so he kept digging into his pocket for the lighter and then replacing it. He could have put the lighter on the table, or I could have bought my own, because this one, a small transparent yellow plastic lighter, was nearly out of fluid and was increasingly difficult to ignite, but our arrangement, the arrangement that surfaced, was that he held on to the lighter and each time I took a cigarette, he lit it for me. If we were outside or sitting close to an open door in a breeze, I would cup my hand around the end of the cigarette and he would place his hand around mine with our fingers overlapping, his thumb resting on mine, so that as I pulled air hard through the cigarette to get it alight, our hands were together in a kind of loose prayer position, protecting a feeble flame.

After two or three bars we drove out to the sea. Probably the intention was to have sex on the beach, but I don't remember now if we did that or not because when we walked back up from the beach something was happening that took over the rest of that night and most of my memories of it. The car park where we left the van from work had been deserted when we arrived, and unlit. Now it was full of noise and light. There were cars all around the edge facing into the centre with engines running and headlights on full beam. Doors were open and people were either sitting inside or leaning on their cars, some were sitting on roofs. I don't know how many cars were there but I guess it was between thirty and forty. The night was cold now, so as well as the exhaust fumes smoking up, there were frosty swirls of air lit up by the headlights like dry ice on a stage.

The show that everyone had gathered to see was what seemed to be a race between two cars driving in fast, tight laps round the space in the middle of the car park. I saw that the contest was not so much a race as a fight and underneath the festival-like mood, the bright lights and the excitement of the crowd, I picked up a bass note of bloodlust. Something gladiatorial was taking place.

The look on Carl's face told me that the situation was not good. We were standing on the edge of whatever it was, and nobody, yet, had noticed us, but our white van – work's white van – was trapped at the back of the car park with no way out except by reversing into the middle of the ring interrupting proceedings and then requiring about six other cars to move to allow us access to the only exit. The white van stood higher than the other vehicles and was the only one actually parked, with its engine off, and facing away from the centre; a tall, pale geek ostracized by a ring of short school bullies. It seemed better not to associate with the weakling.

Carl explained what was going on. They've got two stolen cars, he said, and they are going to trash them. Trash them? Race them, smash them up and set fire to them. It happens here sometimes, he said, I just never thought it would happen tonight. We'll just have to wait it out, I'm sorry. He took off his sweater and passed it to me. It's not your fault! I told him, and gave it back but he insisted – he was good at these small acts of gallantry – and I was grateful because we had been outside for over an hour now and it was cold. I took out a cigarette and Carl did his best to light it for me, but the little yellow lighter spluttered and died. Carl approached a couple standing close to us, who were also huddled together against the cold, and the man lit our cigarettes and his girlfriend smiled at us. With Carl's sweater on and his arms around me, standing at the edge of this thing, smoking like one of the crowd, and with this friendliness from the couple next to us, I relaxed a little and even began to enjoy myself.

Helicopters arrive. Police. They hover over the car park and take it in turns to lower over the crowd pressing us down and out. Some people yell angrily at the helicopters, others scuttle to their cars. We are like a disturbed anthill. Carl takes me by the arm and keeps me close to him and he steers us towards the white van. He has taken control, and I am glad of it, glad of him. A puny strain of music can be heard amid the running engines. There is a queue to get out of the car park, or not a queue, just cars crowding towards the exit and it seems whoever can cram forward fastest gets out first. Carl uses the full height and size of the van and crushes on until we are out. Will they follow? I ask, meaning the helicopters. No, he says. Why aren't there any police in cars? I ask. Because they'd get fucking lynched. Not if they sent enough, I say. There aren't enough, he tells me.

The next day we drove past that car park and, at my request, Carl slowed down because I could see, and was fascinated by, the twisted corpse of one of the cars sacrificed the night before. A blown out front window left a gaping hole like an eye socket and the door had melted over a frame distorted into a jawbone and so the wreckage had the appearance of an enormous blackened sheep skull.

Thirteen

I'm in love with the garden down the street and I think it *is* love, or at the very least a massive crush, because just looking at it makes me want to buy new clothes, eat better, get fit. It's just a little walled garden, but it fills me with desire to reach out; there's something about it I want to claim, or join with, in some way. Everything in it is flourishing. It's wild *and* well tended – I love this combination.

I've been out on the terrace to look at the garden at least once every day since I first saw it. I'm too much of a scaredy-cat to sit on the low wall at the edge so I just stand. And it's a pain dragging my desk back and forth in order to open the doors so I found a new position for the desk, and have left it there. When it gets hotter I'll want to have the terrace doors open more anyway.

Fourteen

I made three mistakes. The first mistake was to kiss Carl in the bar, because that broke the sanctity of what I had with Johnny. The second mistake was to accept the perfume he gave me, because that led to the affair. And the third mistake was to take in his cat, because as long as Molly was living with me, the affair could not be ended cleanly.

Long before I told Johnny about Carl, Carl's girlfriend Katie guessed about me and when she confronted him, he didn't deny it. That same evening Carl set up a bed on the floor in their sitting room. He told me later that their relationship had already dwindled to platonic and that's why Katie accepted his passion for me even though she didn't like it. Neither Katie nor Carl could afford the rent on their own so they agreed that until Katie found somewhere she wanted to move to, they would stay there like that; Katie in the bedroom, Carl on the sitting room floor.

By the time Katie found another place to live, Johnny had left me to go and stay in the yellow room at Robbie's house and I was living alone. Carl found a room somewhere, but there was a dog in the house so he couldn't take Molly. When Carl told me he would have to move, I thought he was going to ask if he could come and live with me, and when he asked instead if I could take Molly for a while I was so relieved that I immediately said yes.

Carl asked me if I was a dog person or a cat person. Neither, I replied, which are you? Both, he said. And then he told me about Scooby, the dog he and his brother had when they were growing up. They loved him dearly from when he was a tiny puppy, but Scooby was a greedy dog and used to eat scraps of food he found on his walks. One day, Scooby found some chicken on the pavement and wolfed it down before Carl could stop him. A bone got stuck in Scooby's throat and he started choking. A small crowd gathered and people were telling Carl what to do, and Carl, who was only twelve and couldn't reach the bone, started getting upset. A man stepped forward, burly, lifted Scooby up and with both arms around his chest, and Scooby's little legs sticking straight out in front like table legs, this man performed the Heimlich manoeuvre and the chicken bone flew out of Scooby's mouth in an arc of spittle. The crowd cheered as the bone hit the pavement and Carl thanked the man and carried his confused dog home. Unfortunately it turned out the man had broken two of Scooby's ribs, and although the vet said the ribs would mend, the dog went into a decline and died.

—

On the last morning at Carl's mother's house, I was *so* ready to leave. I packed up my things, which didn't take long, went outside and smoked what I hoped would be the last of the cheap cigarettes. I went back inside the house to extract Carl. Our Kid was in his pyjamas, which made me want to get out of there even faster. Just before we left, I went to the bathroom and when I came out, Carl took his wallet out of his back pocket, took out several banknotes, folded them and passed them to Our Kid, who thanked him shyly.

I couldn't help thinking that Our Kid's shyness was partly due to me witnessing this transaction, and I wished that Carl had given Our Kid the money while I was in the bathroom. I felt sure that alongside Carl's real interest in Our Kid was his awareness of himself being interested in his brother; that alongside his real concern there was awareness of himself being generous, and that he also had a desire that he perhaps *wasn't* so aware of, which was to demonstrate this generosity in front of other people, in this case, me.

Our director called us both into his office and asked whether we were having an affair. He said it straight, like this: Are you two having an affair? I felt myself turn red in the face. Carl looked straight back at the director, held his gaze, and said, Nope. Now there was a stand-off between the two men: the director knew very well there was something going on between us and Carl knew that he was answering the question correctly because the affair was over by then. We were, I said, but it's finished. It felt awkward saying this to the director in front of Carl because although the affair *was* over, Carl had been coming to my house at night, knocking on my front door, shouting through the letter-box, leaving messages on my answerphone, and making a horrible atmosphere at work. As I said the word 'finished', Carl pulled himself up taller, as if meeting a challenge. It's none of your fucking business anyway, said Carl, under his breath.

Excuse me? said the director, but he'd heard.

I said it's not really any of your business, is it? What we do in our own time?

Correct. But it is my business what you do in work time. The director went on to give examples of misconduct which were so mild compared to some of the things we'd done on company time, with company money, in company cars, that I suddenly felt more relieved than embarrassed. We had got away with it, or at least I had.

The reason Carl didn't ask if he could live with me was because he had already asked me for keys to my flat and I had ignored the request. I had been in the office all day, he elsewhere. He was sitting on my doorstep when I returned home. He'd been there quite a while; it was a warm evening and he had a paper so he didn't mind, he said. I opened up the double doors to the back garden, put my keys on the table, took off my sandals and went into the bathroom to wash my hot grimy feet. Wouldn't it be nice if he had already prepared dinner for us, he called; yes, I called back, though I noticed he wasn't doing anything about dinner now. When I went into the kitchen he was sitting with my key ring round his finger, jangling the keys on the table. I opened the fridge to see what was in it. Maybe I could get keys for here? I'd like that, he said. Would you like some vodka? I replied, as if I hadn't heard him. Not yet then, eh? he said. I remember glancing across at him as I poured out the vodka; he was staring at my keys, passing them through his fingers like prayer beads. But one day she will, he said.

Later that night, when we had nearly finished the vodka, we were lying on a blanket outside, sharing a cigarette. It was dark, or as dark as it ever gets in the city, and because it was hot, everyone's windows and doors were open; household clattering and conversation mingled with the sound of passing cars, occasional sirens, and the distant rumbling of trains and aeroplanes. Next door, somebody was cooking something that smelt good. There was a rare sense of contentment between us, partly achieved by alcohol, but anyway, I was happy to be with him, nestled in the tiny garden, with the evening noises bustling in the air around us.

Carl broke the peace: Love me the way I love you, he

said. OK, I said, but I didn't mean, OK – I'll love you, I meant, OK – I understand what you want. I must have known I was misleading him unless, with the vodka inside me, I thought I *could* love him, but I doubt it. It's more likely I just wanted to keep the evening on track. When I look back on that moment now it makes me sad, the vulnerability of his request, my unspoken refusal. I always knew I would end the affair.

> Don't ask me so soon
> When I'm going to leave you.
> It's only mid-June, a few more weeks
>
> of peonies yet.

> *Deborah Garrison*

I asked Carl why he didn't have a dog, since he had obviously loved Scooby so much. He said he couldn't have another because he still felt guilty when he remembered the look in Scooby's eyes.

I stood there and watched while that fucking cunt crushed him, said Carl.

But you were only twelve, you thought that man was trying to help – he *was* trying to help, I reasoned.

So what? I let him down, said Carl. I said that he hadn't really let his dog down because he hadn't meant to. It makes no difference, said Carl.

—

On a balmy summer's day, Carl and I walked down a tree-lined avenue. We were on our way back to the office after a meeting. I wanted to get straight on the bus but Carl wanted to walk across the park and catch the bus a few stops further on, Come on, he said, it's a beautiful day. So we walked across the park, but the matter wasn't settled: he wanted to linger. At some point he must have unbuttoned his shirt, because I clearly recall my irritation as he dawdled, sunlight on his bare chest, shirt billowing in the breeze, face turned up to the dappled light coming through the trees, drinking it all in. He wanted me to bask with him. Come to Switzerland with me next time, he said with his eyes closed to the sun. I saw then what the special bread meant to Carl. The bread was an emblem of the kind of life he wanted, a life like his friend's in Switzerland, and he wanted that life with me. We held hands, but not peacefully: I dropped his hand: he took mine again: I shifted my briefcase into that hand: he took my briefcase and carried it, took my hand again: I freed myself to tuck my hair behind my ear: again he took hold. It was like a fight – Carl trying to pull me into that moment and me trying to wriggle out of it and run away.

I dream that Carl is banging on my door, demanding entry. He wants a guided tour. I tell him he has to wait five years and then renew his application. When I wake up, the dream is foggy but close enough for me to stay inside it and change the end so that I am telling him something else – something kinder, I think, though exactly what escapes me – and then morning invades, the new ending slides off and I am left with the original dream, with the ending that bothered me.

Carl was always pushing to get in. That he pushed, made the affair happen in the first place, but then he couldn't stop. If he had held back, I could have come forward. Maybe he thought he could make me love him through the sheer force of his feelings for me. I felt guilty that I didn't return Carl's love. The least I could do was to look after his cat for a while.

Occasionally, I decide to leave things out of the story. I notice that the things I want to omit are usually my own base actions and low words. I would include them, I think, if I believed their inclusion was imperative to getting to the truth.

I changed one detail: the green shirt that Carl gave me long before the first kiss and that Johnny cut to shreds with a knife once he knew about the affair was not a green shirt but a grey jacket. I changed it because a shirt is more personal, and I wanted to bring out the intimacy of Carl's gift. Also, a shirt has been on someone's back, next to skin, and so the act of knifing a shirt seems more violent than cutting up a jacket and I wanted to show the strength of Johnny's anger when he found out about Carl.

Things that may sound invented aren't. There really is a place called the Forest of Maibie, and I really did wander around it wondering what to do. Carl really did climb that tower in the ruined castle with me at the top, gazing out of the window. Johnny's best friend really was called Don Juan. He really did milk clouds. And I really did buy an expensive pair of satin shoes that looked like glass slippers.

Also – it occurs to me that there may not have been a dog in the house Carl was moving to: I never visited him there so I never saw one, and I don't think he ever mentioned it again. It's possible that Carl invented the dog just so he could get Molly in with me, as a kind of anchor.

I knew what Carl meant about the special bread. I visited a friend of a friend in Madrid, a woman my age I'd never met before, and I had to wait a couple of hours at her apartment, by myself, while she finished work before meeting me there and showing me round the city.

She lived alone in a small apartment at the top of an old building. I was enthralled by the aspects of her life that were on display – the expensive hand cream on her bedside table, postcards and little notes in Spanish stuck around the mirror in her bathroom, chocolate truffles in a gold box in the fridge, the view over the streets from her kitchen window.

What stays with me most, though, is her bowl of almonds on a low glass table. It seemed incredible to me that it was possible to live like this; in this particular city, surrounded by these particular things; the sight of that bowl of almonds had a revelatory effect: Oh! You mean it can be done like *this*?

Fifteen

Apart from the fact that I didn't like cats, there were practical problems with having Molly come and live with me. One, there was no cat flap for her to get outside and I didn't want one installed since it was a temporary arrangement. Two, I did not keep regular hours to come back and feed her and let her out at the same time each day. And three, once out in the garden, how could I ensure that she didn't run away, or get lost, or run over, or kidnapped?

Look, Carl said, I live on the fourth floor, there's no cat flap because there's no outside, and I don't keep regular hours either. You just change her water and put her food down in the mornings: done. I'll bring the litter tray and a sack of litter: done. She never misses, but we could lay the tray on newspaper just in case. Charming, I said, already regretting the arrangement.

I'll empty the tray and change the litter every time I'm at yours, which is almost every night, isn't it? Done. Sorted. No problem. His chirpiness was making my heart heavy.

Well, what about letting her go outside? How do I know she'll come back?

I take her for walks on a lead, he said.

But she's a cat, not a dog!

So? It works: she likes it.

She likes it, I repeated, deadened.

The period after the affair lasted longer than the affair itself, and was at least as intense. When Carl was bombarding me with phone calls and unanswered night-time visits, his excuse was that he wanted to check up on Molly. He claimed I didn't know how to look after her properly and that he was sure I was mistreating her. Most of the messages he left on my answerphone followed a pattern: they started off fairly normally; he would say he was calling to check that Molly had had her walk today, or that she had eaten her food, or that I was cleaning the litter tray regularly, or giving her fresh water. He would make his enquiry, and then ask how I was, say he was missing me, that he wished we were still together, that he knew he could make me happy if only I would give him another chance. At this point there would usually be a silence. I don't know what happened to him during these silences but I imagine him spiralling down and down until he hit the bottom of his despair and his anger rose up because next he would start muttering insults or making demands. On some messages he was yelling down the phone by the end of the call, making threats I couldn't hear properly because he was shouting so loudly that the words were distorted.

The first time Carl left a ranting message, I called him straight away and said I would bring Molly back to him. I was careful not to say that he could come and collect her because I'd already experienced difficulty getting him out of my flat on one or two occasions. But Carl said he couldn't take Molly back because of the dog in the house he was staying in. I suggested that one of his friends looked after Molly instead of me; I should have insisted. I should have taken Molly to work and let him deal with her; if Carl couldn't house her, he could have found a cattery. I could have put her in a cattery myself. But it's all very well saying these things now. I kept Molly. I had my reasons: Carl and I had to see each other in the office every day, I felt a responsibility to keep work moving forward, Carl was volatile. Everyone was being very careful around him because they knew that I had finished our affair. I thought it was up to me to contain his anger and so I assumed the role of bomb-disposal technician. Also, I was fearful of what would happen if he did blow up. I suppose I thought it was easier to put up with the controlled explosions on my answer-machine than risk full-scale collateral damage. As well as this, I had grown fond of Molly. At the end of each message Carl sounded savage, and my instinct was to protect Molly. But I am getting carried away. Carl adored Molly; he would never have harmed her.

Maybe keeping hold of Molly was the biggest mistake I made. It confused matters, blurred the ending. While Carl and I were together it was so intense that maybe he couldn't accept it was over so quickly. Or perhaps there was something about the way I broke up with him that he couldn't accept, something unclear in the way I said it or about the words I chose. Perhaps he needed to hear an unequivocal answer to his question. Are you ever going to love me the way I love you?

Sixteen

I have been up at night and unable to write during the day. It's June already and extremely hot. July will only be worse and I hate August (such a dead month). The nights are noisy, full of drunks and people fighting and sirens wailing so I close the doors at night which means the air has no movement. I have tried earplugs, I have tried sleeping with the doors closed *and* earplugs but it is no use. The slightest noise is an irritation, regardless of how many layers away it is.

> Past midnight, a weeknight, I'm still
> sitting in a carved out, windowless place
> off Eighth Avenue. The heat
>
> outside's a piston
> insisting itself into the dead
> center of August. Nobody
>
> smokes anymore.
>
> *Alison Jarvis*

This morning I tried to deal with some of the stuff that's been sitting around since I moved in. I was not really unpacking, just moving things around. It's a bad habit, leaving things in boxes.

I did unwrap my pictures though, and decided where they should go. So now each has a home, and is leaning on the wall below that spot, waiting. I have a drill. I know how to use it. Perhaps tomorrow.

After that, I went out to check on the garden. It looks a bit tired from this heat, but clearly someone is watering it. I took a cushion out and snapped bubble wrap and drank too much coffee. One of the builders was leaning out of the top right hand window, smoking. I watched hungrily. From time to time I will trail a smoker in the street.

Carl taught me how to blow smoke rings, which I loved doing. I remember showing Johnny and Juan one night, Johnny sulked because I was smoking but Juan was impressed and told me that the Yámanas people used smoke signals to communicate and that Magellan saw these fires, which inspired him to name the landscape Tierra del Fuego. Juan also told me about the Magellanic Clouds, two galaxies visible only in the southern hemisphere. (Imagine – two whole galaxies invisible to half the world!) I teased him: If you milked a Magellanic cloud, would you get stars?

Seventeen

Each morning I had the same thing for breakfast: two large cups of black filter coffee and two slices of white toast, one with butter, one with butter and marmalade. I ate the buttered slice first and the slice with marmalade second – for pudding, as it were. I had to have the right cup; a wide-brimmed white cup, and the coffee had to be very hot. I always reheated the coffee in a pan for the second cup. I used to love the way the steam rose from the coffee, the way the butter melted into the hot toast leaving tiny gold puddles on the plate. Carl noticed my morning routine; I suppose that's why, for my birthday, he gave me the proper coffee pot and the cup and saucer with the image of that long limbed woman draped around them. It was thoughtful of him, but they didn't fit: I used my breakfast to help me feel like myself in the mornings, the woman on the cup was too languid. After a pint of coffee, I certainly didn't feel languid. Whenever Carl was there, I made coffee in the new pot and drank from the cup and saucer he gave me, but if I was alone I reverted to the old plastic filter, ceramic jug and my favourite white cup.

I had barred myself from approaching my sister for support, first because of her accident and then because after her recovery she had a change in fortune: she landed a new job, highly paid, and met a smooth new man. She was so smart, all of a sudden, that I felt left behind. I felt sorry for myself: I had first kissed Carl in the aftermath of her accident and because I was still involved with Carl after she had moved on I seemed to think it was me who bore the scars, not her. It was not that she had become too grand to listen to my problems, but that I now saw her as too grand to tell them to. Also, I was scared of what she would say. Because she liked Johnny, I assumed she would say I was better off with him and imagined her telling me he was a diamond and I'd never find another man like him. This is what she actually said: If you really have to leave Johnny, go ahead – but do it by your own strength, not through this other guy; he sounds like a nightmare.

The other day I complained to her about not sleeping: It would be all right, I think, if I could relax in the day . . . tend to something, or get on with this writing, but I am not even doing that.

Why not make your own garden, on the roof? she said, brightly.

Instantly I felt even more frustrated because I'd already *had* that idea, it was mine – she just said it first.

On that trip to China, during the flight, I felt as though I was shrinking from fear of going to a place where I didn't speak the language and couldn't read the script. I arrived in Beijing and boarded another flight straight away for a far off province. I decided I would cope by staying in one place, getting to know it little by little, but that isn't what I did.

Very early one morning, when it was still dark, I entered a large bus station. There were many buses preparing to leave. There were plenty of signs but none of them in English, and plenty of people but if any of them spoke English, I didn't know. An English-speaking teacher I met had helped me buy a ticket the day before, but now I had to find the right bus. The teacher had written the name of my destination on a piece of paper. Underneath the script, I had written how the name sounded, or at least how it sounded to me when the teacher said it. I went to each bus stand until I found a sign that matched my piece of paper, then I approached a young woman standing under the sign and showed her my piece of paper, and my ticket, and tried to repeat the name, and she smiled and nodded, so I got on that bus. The young woman went away, which worried me; I had assumed she was making the same journey and when I saw her turn and walk off I felt a pang of regret sharper than when Johnny had said goodbye at the airport.

The bus journey was sixteen hours. Most of it was on big smooth roads, and every so often there were road signs, in Mandarin, so I had no way of knowing which towns and cities the bus was heading for, nor how near or far they were. A nut of anxiety hardened in my stomach each time we passed a sign: Was I on the right bus? Had I made myself clear to the young woman at the bus stand? Had I pronounced the name well enough? What if I was travelling sixteen hours in the opposite direction? In the grip of these fears, I would turn to my neighbours on the bus and repeat the name of my destination to them, and produce my piece of paper and my ticket as if they were evidence of my existence. I tried to make a question of the place-name, but I wasn't exactly sure how questions sounded in Mandarin, and it occurred to me that, as far as my neighbours were concerned, and possibly as far as the young woman at the bus stand had been concerned, maybe all I was doing was asserting the existence of a place named Songjiazhuang, without, actually, making it clear that I wanted to go there.

After several panics, I realized – these fears are making me ludicrous! I am on the right bus, I said to myself sternly, and left my neighbours in peace. If someone approaches you in a bus station, or on a bus, and shows you a ticket and a place name, this means they want to go to that place. And you can indicate if it is the right bus, or not. There is no language barrier involved. Am I going in the right direction? This is a question that doesn't always need to be asked, or answered, in words.

I found much of what I needed in books. There were certain passages that I read over and over, because they shed light on my situation and offered a way through. The most significant time this happened was two weeks after the first kiss with Carl, on a small draughty train across country at dusk. I had been trying to concentrate on Johnny, trying to get Carl out of my mind, but I found a poem that so thrilled me, I could barely get to the end before I started reading it again, and then I held off from a third visit because I had a sense that if I carried on hammering this poem with the force of my reading, something might happen. There was a sudden sense of vertigo, and I knew I was on the brink of letting myself fall.

I stared out of the dirty window into the darkening sky for a long time before I dared read it again.

The poem was about the myth of Daphne and Apollo, in which Apollo sees Daphne, and decides he wants her.

Daphne turns Apollo down but he pursues her, and she escapes him by transforming herself into a tree.

> And how I ran from him!
>
> The trees reached out to me,
> I silvered
> and I quivered.
> I shook out
> my foil of quick leaves.
>
> He snouted past.
> What a fool I was!
>
> *Eavan Boland*

In the poem, Daphne gives Apollo the slip; she stays perfect – and regrets it. My own sister urged me to stay away from Carl. But Daphne's advice to me was this:

> Fall. Stumble.
> Rut with him.
> His rough heat
> will keep you warm.

When my train reached the city that night, I phoned Carl from the station to say, I have to see you, then drove miles to see him for five minutes outside his block of flats, with Katie waiting up in their bed for him, thinking he was putting out the rubbish, and Johnny waiting way across the city for me in ours, thinking my train had been delayed.

What I felt, when I saw Carl waiting for me, was overwhelming gratitude, a surge of something like love. (Could it have been love? What was I grateful for?) Carl stood a little way away from the deep-set doorway of his apartment block, so that the building offered him no protection against the sharp spring wind. Shoulders slightly hunched in the cold night, fists shoved deep in his two front pockets. He wore a baggy red T-shirt, no jacket, familiar looking blue jeans and old white trainers. I stopped the car, unfastened my seat belt, opened the door, but before I could get out, he was in, and we were kissing as though the kissing were a continuation of something that speaking would interrupt. I remember the chill on Carl's arms, his stubble scraping my face, not in an unpleasant way, and how warm his mouth was.

This, the second time we kissed, was the only time I went to him. Later, when our affair was going full tilt, he told me that because of what I had said to him the day after the first kiss in the bar – that it was a mistake and must never happen again – if I hadn't gone to him, he would have stayed away.

I am beginning to find that I don't believe in mistakes. They are choices.

—

Johnny always used to ask me what I had had for lunch, if I hadn't had lunch with him, and I was pleased to be asked and pleased to tell him, probably because he gave me the sense he was living my life with me, watching over me, interested in every detail; I suppose it gave me the illusion that I was not alone.

I don't always notice the ridiculous things I do, but on that bus ride in China, perhaps because it was such a long way and because I didn't have anyone to talk to, I saw that even after I had stopped pestering my neighbours I was still looking out for road signs, trying to make out distinct groupings of text that I could assume were place names followed by the distance in kilometres. I took comfort from that, though it wasn't anything. I'm on my way, was the comfort I took. And once I noticed that I was watching out for signs that I didn't understand, I realized that it was pretty funny, and then I started to enjoy the trip: I was present on the bus, looking out at the long smooth road and the expanse of flat land all around. It didn't matter that the landscape was boring. It didn't even matter that I wasn't sure of my destination. I felt alive: I am here.

This was the same feeling I got when I was around Carl: I loved what I became, which wasn't all good but it was fresh and vibrant and not smoothly dull. I felt more real.

—

Johnny's mother was grand. At least, she sounded grand. When I first met her, at a smart tearoom in Johnny's university town, I asked her if she had driven there and must have looked startled at her reply, which sounded like, Ears, but was, Yes. Another time, I was staying at Johnny's parents' house and we were thinking where to go that evening. Why don't you take her to Cairns? Johnny's mother suggested. I was expecting a Scottish restaurant, so I was surprised when it turned out to be Indian: Kahn's.

But there was an episode that made me wonder if I was as exotic to Carl as Johnny's mother was to me. When we visited Our Kid, Carl stopped the car just before we reached the house so that I could buy cigarettes. I went into the newsagents, but they didn't stock my brand. I came out of the shop and tried the garage over the road: again, no luck. I went back to the car.

What's up? asked Carl.

They don't have any Marlboro Lights, I said, can we go somewhere else?

Ha! You won't get Marlboro fucking Lights round here, he said.

I went back into the newsagents and armed myself with the wrong cigarettes, just enough to last me until I got back to Marlboro country.

—

Now I see how I used habits to hold myself together, how routine can bind identity. Then, no matter how clearly I saw that the strong black coffee was going to strip the inside of my mouth and make me parched for the rest of the day, or how the toast would taste of nothing and give me no real nourishment, I had to have them. I couldn't skip breakfast because it was my habit to have breakfast and I couldn't have tried something else because that meant thinking of and then buying other things. Making these changes would have taken something I didn't have. So I kept on with the black coffee and toast even though I didn't really want them.

I once wrote down something Sylvia Plath said, copied it from a newspaper article, which may have been a review of a Ted Hughes book. I can't find that place in my notebook now, but I remember what she said almost word for word because it chimed with things I thought. She said something like this: I don't want to become an uninspired, self-rationalizing, stay-at-home housewife while my husband grows intellectually and professionally. I don't want to submerge my biggest aspirations, my embarrassing desires, refuse to face myself.

The myth with Johnny was called 'Domestic Bliss'. There was real love there but it became smothered by cosiness. Ingredients of the myth included a nicely furnished home, holidays abroad, children, his career first, mine second. In short, asking each other what we had had for lunch every day of our lives.

The myth with Carl was called 'Perfect Woman'. It was exciting, at first. Ingredients included being constantly admired, a lot of sex, but it was a prequel to the other myth, whose frame boxed me in. I had to rip the canvas, elbow my way out: *Fall. Stumble.*

> I have written this
> so that
> in the next myth
> my sister
> will be wiser.
>
> Let her learn from me:
> the opposite of passion
> is not virtue
> but routine.
>
> *Eavan Boland*

I grew tired of Johnny asking what I had had for lunch. After four years, it stopped being cute. So one day, trying to keep the irritation out of my voice, I answered: Look, I don't want to play that game any more. Oh, he said, crestfallen. He never asked me again.

—

Apollo is running fast, breathing hard; he has been hunting for days; he is tired and hungry, yet his appetite for you is wearing off. There are millions of stars in the sky. There are others he could have. Perhaps it is not only you. He is no longer running, no longer searching. Apollo, whose slowing step you recognize from troubled dreams, is about to walk away.

It was wonderful to be hotly pursued. I enjoyed the chase so much that I would have liked it to go on and on, but each situation has its own limits: eventually one party gets tired; gives in, goes away. The thrill of the chase is partly made up of wanting to be caught, but there comes a point where you do, actually, have to be caught – or escape. You have to choose.

Eighteen

I waited ages for a bus this morning and I am late to meet my sister at the garden centre. By the time I arrive, she is caustic. People are trundling round, filling their time. In order to distance ourselves from the Sunday drivers, we are businesslike as we select pots and plants and appropriate compost. I choose geraniums, thrift, valerian, some poppies and sweet peas, a cystus.

It's quite late to be starting a garden, I say to the man at the till.

It's always a good time to plant, he replies, which I find reassuring.

On the way out I see a lemon tree in a large earthenware pot with a white glaze that makes it look all the more Mediterranean. The leaves are a lovely shade of green and curl elegantly at the tips. I love the faint citrus smell and there are two green lemons.

Hang on, I say.

My sister, who has had enough, rolls her eyes.

The nice man at the till comes over and tells me it is possible to keep a lemon tree in London but that I will have to bring it inside for the autumn and winter.

What's the point, then? says Emily. How are you going to move it? You won't be able to lift it on your own.

You could have it on a little trolley, the man says.

Now my sister argues with him: There's also a step. A trolley won't get over it without being lifted and she won't be able to do that on her own.

I could get a ramp, I say.

She sums up: A trolley, a ramp, and a tree that has to be inside for six months of the year.

It *is* a lot of work, the man concedes. My sister gives me a triumphant look.

I buy the lemon tree.

Nineteen

There is what I remember, what I know, what I think, and what I imagine. Then there is how these things look, sound and feel when they are written down – the way, sometimes, the written down version seems to take away from the truth rather than add to it. I am not telling the story so much as finding it, making it.

But I don't want to make up too much. Right from the start, from the first kiss with Carl, there has been pain, for Johnny, for Carl, and for me. I tried running away from the pain, and that didn't work; and now, writing, it seems to me that if I invent too many parts of the story, it is the same as running away. But if I stay still, sometimes I see how I could describe a part of what happened. And if I manage to write that part down, it might lead, like a narrow path between tall buildings, to another part of the story, and if I can write *that* part, another alley appears, and in this way I follow the story as if finding my way round the dark quarter of some strange city. But there are a lot of dead ends. When I find that I am stuck, surrounded by brick walls and locked doors, it is not because the story has dried up at that point: the alleyways have stopped appearing because my writing has not been true enough.

Watching the builders opposite might be a form of running away, but it's difficult not to because they are right in front of me, and so interesting – not as individuals (though I have a soft spot for the young one) but as a group and as parts of a group. We have a relationship, of sorts, unequal, as relationships often are, because they have many ways of avoiding work – of which looking at me is one – while for me they are the chief distraction.

I make mistakes about them, though. For example, just now one was standing on the very top of the roof with his back to me, his arms stretched out to each side like Christ on the cross, and for a moment I thought he was going to jump and then I realized he was measuring distance with his hands, and the other day I saw one through a half open window and I thought he was praying but it turned out he was blowing his nose.

I remember arriving at Carl's mother's house, a terraced house on a busy road, the doors and window frames painted in a bright red that clashed with the earthier red of the bricks. The front door was locked and Carl didn't have a key. He banged on the door with his fist yelling, Hello! at the house. Maybe he's not in, I said. He's always in, said Carl. He pushed back the flap of the letterbox and shouted through the hole, Oi! Dozy bastard! Come on! Carl's brother eventually shuffled to the door, unlocked it from the inside, opened it, then turned and walked away down a hall. It was the middle of the afternoon but he was wearing pale blue pyjamas and the soles of his feet were dirty. What have you got the door locked for? asked Carl, walking after his brother. I went in, closing the door behind me. I haven't been out, said Carl's brother.

Since when?

Dunno.

Christ, said Carl. I followed the two brothers into a kitchen. Carl sat down at a small square table, in front of a dirty ashtray and an empty glass with a ring of milk at the bottom of it. Displaced, his brother stood by the back door and stared out of the window at the backs of other houses. He had the smell of desperation about him – a smell I know because I have had it, although I didn't have it then. I couldn't help noticing a couple of stains on the pale blue pyjamas, around the crotch. His toenails were long and yellowy. He was taller than Carl, skinny, with dark blond hair hanging lank around his face, ears poking through; like a long-term unemployed Jesus.

Put the kettle on, then, said Carl.

OK, said his brother, not moving.

I thought Our Kid's real name might have been John, or Paul, but now I realize I have nothing to base this on and that I may have been thinking about the last Pope, or one of the Beatles. Most of the time we were there – two nights and three days – Our Kid played his guitar in the front room in his blue pyjamas. I think he had an amp plugged into the back of the television, but I could be wrong about that too.

I made another mistake just now. A builder was leaning out of a window and I saw what I took to be a skull cap on his head and I was thinking how I hadn't seen this before and began to wonder what percentage of builders are Jewish but I hadn't finished this thought when I realized it was a face mask pulled up onto his hair.

It was early summer – June, I think – when Molly moved in, a strange event: Carl and I trading gestures over the top of her small hard head as though she were a new currency we were dealing in. I bought Molly a present, a wicker basket with a red and white checked cushion, Molly bought me flowers and wine. I *thanked* her. Carl was visibly pleased by this exchange. I felt like screaming. But I went along with it because I didn't want to upset Carl: already I was posturing; already I was boxed in. This is lying: acting one thing while feeling another. This is boxing oneself in.

Carl showed Molly round the flat, giving her instructions: here is the bed – don't go on the bed; here is the bathroom – don't jump up on the shelf and knock everything off; here is the sofa – don't scratch the legs; here is the kitchen – don't lick the butter. And here is the kitchen window: this will be closed so you won't be able to jump out. This last instruction was for me.

Carl wanted to show Molly the garden. He attached a slender velvet lead to her collar and asked me to unlock the back doors. I felt like a jailer with my big bunch of keys, letting the prisoner into the exercise yard. Carl carried Molly down the steps, set her down on the dry grass and followed her as she padded and poked around at the end of her lead.

Why don't you let her off the lead for a little while?

Because I don't want her to run away.

I organized a work event on a wooden sailing ship on the river. The ship was moored, but the motion of the river slammed the boat against the concrete siding and water slapped against the sides. This was after I had broken up with Carl, during his angry phase. When all the guests had gone home and we were clearing up, I found myself alone with him in the cabin on the lower deck. There was a big stack of brown plastic barrels that were meant to look like wooden kegs of ale or rum and we had to unload them from the ship into a van. Carl was on a stepladder, taking the barrels from the top. To begin with he was passing them to another member of our team, but this person went off, probably because he didn't want to be alone with Carl and me, and so Carl started passing them to me, roughly. After a little while, I said, You're passing those barrels as if you want to hit me with one of them, and Carl replied, without looking at me, If I wanted to hit you, I'd just fucking do it. I don't know why I stayed in the room after he said this. I don't remember feeling afraid. I just remember noticing, each time he shoved one at me, how nobody could ever really mistake these barrels for wood.

A couple of days after this event on the ship, Carl was to go away on business. I couldn't wait for him to leave. I helped him get ready for his trip, packing a box with a slide projector, slides, brochures to hand out, road map. I carried the box down to the car park and loaded it into the back of the company car. He didn't thank me. He shut the boot with unnecessary force and went back into the building to get his jacket. I waited in the reception area and when he came down the stairs, I opened the door for him. Bye, I said, and Carl snorted through his nose like a bull. As I closed the door after him, my fingers released the latch so that when the door closed, it locked.

What are you doing? asked the receptionist, irritated. I looked at her. You locked the door! Nobody can get in. Oh, sorry, I said, unlocking the door and putting it on the latch again. I went back upstairs to my desk, bewildered by the action my own hand had taken; I didn't plan to lock the door, I didn't know I was doing it. So that was a shock. My body felt heavy, there was the beginning of nausea, and then I knew: I am frightened of Carl.

It doesn't happen from the head down. That's not how it is. You don't always decide to do something and then do it, or decide not to do something and then not do it. And this doesn't mean you are not responsible, it means responsibility is wider than you thought and includes all of the choices you made even if they were made by your hands or your feet or your lips before they registered in your head.

I disobeyed my instruction: I left the kitchen window open. Only a crack. But one night while I was sleeping and Carl was in Switzerland, Molly escaped.

Towards the end of that long bus journey in China, when it was dark, and the other passengers were slumped shapes, sleeping, the bus came to a sprawling town and stopped. I checked in to a hotel near the bus terminal and had just unlocked the door of a room on the eighth floor when there was a power cut: sudden and complete, the whole town in darkness. Not knowing when or if the power would return, but knowing the contents of my small bag as well as I once knew my way back from school, I found my torch and lit my way to bed, and there, far from home, in a blank room, in an anonymous hotel, in a dark town, on a huge continent, I settled down to sleep, feeling as buoyant and hard-soft as driftwood.

The driftwood feeling is this: I am just bobbing along in a vast and excellent world. I didn't have this kind of contentment all the time, only in sitting down moments here and there, but I knew it, and always believed it would come again.

Molly was not allowed to drink milk. She didn't get enough exercise because she was only allowed outside on a lead, and a vet had advised Carl to keep her weight down. I sometimes used to eat a bowl of cereal for dinner, and once, when Carl wasn't there, Molly jumped up onto the kitchen counter and started to lap the milk in the bottom of the bowl. I let her finish it, and after that I gave her one secret saucer every day, though I always bought her skimmed milk.

About to leave for his climbing in Switzerland, Carl almost decided not to go:

I'll miss you so much.

But I'll be here when you get back.

I don't want to leave you.

But it's only for five days. (Please go!)

I want to stay with you here, in this bed.

But *(Please go!)* . . .

I fetched a black marker pen from my workbag, took the duvet and pillows off the bed and had him lie flat. I drew around him with the pen, carefully so as not to tickle. Afterwards we looked at the outline of his body on the white sheet.

There – you see? You will still be with me.

I did not sleep with the outline of Carl's body. The night I drew around him it seemed like a fine thing to do (anything to get him away to Switzerland and give me a few days off) but the next morning, after I kissed him goodbye at my door, I went straight into the bedroom and stripped the bed and put the sheet in the washing machine on a very hot cycle. The outline of his body was too spooky, like one of those chalk outlines of bodies you see where there has been a death; someone has been knocked down, or jumped, or fallen.

I thought Carl was sensitive to the balance between us but he can't have been, otherwise he would surely have noticed the false notes I played. I feel bad about this episode now because it amounts to a lie. Perhaps Carl did notice the disharmony and ignored it, preferring to believe I was genuine in my affection for him, or hoping that my affection would, in time, become genuine.

—

Molly went on my bed all the time. She didn't use the wicker basket once – I ended up keeping shoes in it. I would come home from work and find her fast asleep in a square of sunlight on the new white duvet, bright specks of dust floating above her warm, compact little body, a sunbeam shining down on her like a spotlight. Quietly, I would take off my shoes, lie down next to Molly, close my eyes, and rest.

At my flat one morning, alone, I was about to spread my two slices of toast when I noticed something odd about the butter. All the edges had been blunted. And there was an imprint, as though a nail file had been pressed into the smooth yellow surface. Then I understood: this was no nail file; this was the work of a raspy cat tongue.

Molly did other things Carl had told her not to. She jumped up onto the bathroom shelf, the one that Johnny made, and knocked things off, including the perfume that Carl gave me, which I was still wearing at that point. She sharpened her claws on the legs of my sofa. She pestered me for bits of whatever I was eating. She walked, purring, along the length of the kitchen counter, shedding hair. She dribbled on my clothes and dug her claws into my thighs before settling on my lap. But I could forgive her anything for those late afternoon naps in a sunbeam, her peaceful slumber an invitation to another world.

—

Carl showed me his mother's room. There was a deep pile cream carpet, white furniture, and a king-sized bed with a pink eiderdown. Carl wanted me to look round the room, urged me to open cupboards, drawers, the wardrobe and look inside. From this, I inferred that he wanted me to ask questions about her, so I did, and I picked up her things with what I hoped was the right mixture of curiosity and respect, handling each item with exaggerated care as though it was an exhibit in a museum. In the wardrobe, shoes and boots were placed neatly under the clothes. There were lots of dresses. Something about the garments hanging loosely reminded me of Our Kid in his pale blue pyjamas, his skinny body hanging off his bones; there was nothing *in* him, no agency, or if there was, it was buried deep. Other artefacts; white lace doilies under a set of three white china boxes with a pale orange floral pattern on the lids; airport blockbusters on a shelf; curlers and a hairdryer in the top drawer of the white dressing table; in another drawer, the brown glass bottles that contained the pills she had taken to kill herself.

There was something staged about the mother's room. She had been dead for years. The room was arranged to look 'exactly as she left it'. And yet the wastepaper bin was empty, the hairbrush had no stray hairs on it, there was no dust anywhere, and on the bedside table there was a thick paperback with a bookmark sticking out of it about three quarters of the way through. The room was constructed, like a film set, to tell a story and it certainly conjured up a presence: you felt that at any minute she could walk in. Maybe if it had been my dead mother, I too would have built her a shrine. When we went out, Carl closed the door softly so as not to disturb the spirit of the room, but the spirit of the room – or something wider – had already disturbed me.

The unfinished book puzzles me: If it was no good then why had she read so much of it, and, having got so far with it, wouldn't she want to finish it first?

When I discovered Molly was gone, I worried about how to tell Carl that she had escaped through an open window. If I was responsible for losing his cat, I would owe him and he would have power over me. I imagined him hissing, I *told* you about the window, and what would he do then? I had seen his anger ignite over much smaller matters, like being barred from the stately home or not being invited to meet my friends, so what would he do if I lost his beloved cat? But then Molly slipped in through the kitchen window with the grace of an otter dipping through water, and my relief was huge.

Twenty

I'm ending all of it, said Carl, standing on the edge of the roof of the office, six floors above the empty car park. It was early evening; most of the staff had already left. I had been waiting all day to tell him, again. It was no use telling him at my flat because then I had to get him to leave, and that would be difficult. I thought a public place was out of the question because he would probably cry, or shout, as he had done when I tried to break up with him before. My mistake was to think this mattered. I should have dumped him in a crowd and disowned his reaction. But I decided to tell him after work, on the roof. I lured him up there with the offer of a cigarette break. I knew I had to say the words quickly, and then leave. I lit a cigarette and thought: By the time I finish smoking this, I will be rid of him.

Breaking up with Carl had taken weeks because I tried to do it gently. Carl argued, protested, cried, sulked, pleaded, bought gifts, made apologies. I said things like: I need to be on my own for a while, I can't settle into another relationship straight away, It's not you, it's me. These clichés seemed true enough, and it was easier than saying: It's you. I was using clichés as a way of distancing myself from him, but it didn't work. I said they were true enough, but they were not, they didn't hold enough truth and so they were not believable. I had to tell Carl: It's you: I don't want to be with you: I don't love you. And that's when he threatened to jump off the roof.

While we were at their mother's house, Carl tried to take Our Kid in hand. He decided they needed a clear out. My role was to witness this. Carl climbed into the loft and handed down dusty bags to Our Kid who lined them up along the landing. There were tied up black bin liners, small plastic bags, boxes, a couple of empty suitcases, a sewing machine, an artificial Christmas tree and a fold-up exercise bike. Our Kid passed the vacuum cleaner up to Carl and we heard Carl and the vacuum going back and forth across the small floor. While we waited on the landing for Carl to finish, Our Kid did not open any of the bags or look in any of the boxes; he did not look at the line of stuff at all. He leaned against the wall and smoked. Carl and the vacuum came down the ladder. Right! said Carl. We're going to the tip.

Carl loaded the bags, boxes, suitcases and Christmas tree into the back of the van. He had a lot of energy that day, in contrast to Our Kid, who was floppy and had none. Carl started the ignition, put some loud music on and leant forward on the steering wheel while we climbed in; Our Kid in the middle, near the gear stick, me next. I noticed that Our Kid wasn't wearing his seat belt but I didn't say anything about that. At the tip, Our Kid dematerialized so I helped Carl throw everything into the gaping yellow container. It didn't take long. Our Kid was back in his place in the van, with the Christmas tree on the floor between his feet. Carl leant into the van and reached for it. Our Kid picked it up quickly – the quickest I'd seen him move – and gripped it in his two hands like a staff, all the while looking straight ahead. Sensing trouble, I walked round to the back of the van and lit a cigarette.

While I was trying to break up with him nicely, Carl used to find excuses to talk to me all the time; invent reasons for meetings; call me on the internal phone and entreat me to have lunch with him; smoke cigarettes on the fire escape by my desk and chat to me as I was trying to work. But his emotions changed direction after he threatened to commit suicide. He switched from pleading with me to get back together with him to raging because I wouldn't. He stopped talking to me and if he did have to talk to me, he wouldn't look at me. We were barely speaking to each other even though his desk was near mine and we worked on the same floor. This was when he started leaving threatening phone messages. At first I was relieved that I didn't have to listen to his whining any more, but after a week of coming home to poison on my answerphone I was anxious. His anger was so great; the phone alone surely couldn't contain it. I didn't see how he could continue to force his anger down the puny plastic line without some damage.

One morning Carl asked if he could talk to me for a minute. It was the first time in two weeks he had addressed me directly without venom. He pulled his chair over to my desk and confided this: on his way home the night before, he was coming up an escalator and there were two men standing just below him. One of the men said something offensive to Carl and when Carl challenged him he didn't retract it so Carl punched this man in the face and the man fell all the way down to the bottom of the escalator. I don't remember what I said to him in response, but whatever it was, it didn't make any difference: within two days he started leaving horrible messages again.

The artificial Christmas tree had a star at the top. You could see that the tree once had shine and sparkle and thick tinsel boughs, but now the star was crumpled, the silver had faded to a greyish-white, some of the branches were bent, and there was dust in the rivulets that stood for wood grain in the brown plastic base. Still, I hoped to hear the engine start and that we would return to the mother's house with

Our Kid clutching that tree, pathetic though it was. But as I stubbed out the cigarette, I saw Carl emerge from the cab with the Christmas tree in his fist and a grim look on his face and hurl the thing after all the other stinking rubbish into the depths of the black hole.

Attempts to hang on are inelegant – I see this, I do – it's just that making Our Kid let go of that tree was an act of violence and, even though she was Carl's mother too, it seemed sacrilegious. At the house Our Kid trickled into his room. I barely saw him after that, except at Carl's funeral.

Maybe Carl's mother wasn't even reading that book. Maybe Our Kid or Carl placed it there and placed the bookmark inside as part of the film set of her room; a relic – like the skinny Christmas tree, and Johnny's records, and the photograph of Carl that I kept hidden. Relics are markers of loss: first there is the day and then the day is over and you have a photograph, a T-shirt, a memory. Years go by and you misplace the photograph, throw out the faded shirt and your memory falters. More years pass and the memory fades too. Losing memories is fitting. Loss follows loss. We build histories with surviving memories – whole civilizations constructed from lost days.

Carl went into his brother's room and came out with dirty laundry including the pale blue pyjamas Our Kid had been wearing since we arrived. Our Kid emerged in jeans and a sweatshirt. Later, in Carl's mother's kitchen, I emptied the wash into a white plastic basket, took it outside and started pegging out the clothes. Normally there is something peaceful about hanging out a wash, like the mood I sometimes slip into when I'm writing; an idea comes to mind, presenting itself as a kind of line; I peg words onto it, take some off, change things around, repeat this process until the words describe, as closely as they can, the idea that I am trying to communicate. But on this occasion I remember a growing sense of apprehension. I hung up the pale blue pyjamas, aware of the absence of their mother. I didn't want to keep going as Carl's perfect woman. Yet here I was, hanging out his brother's socks, vests and underwear, and I felt I was intruding on the sorrow of the household because I was wrongfully occupying a role I didn't even want, and so hanging out this particular wash on the line became a form of trespass.

Carl punching the man to the bottom of the escalator was on my mind all day. I decided to go to the station where the punch had taken place. There might be one of those big yellow crime signs asking for information about the violent incident on the escalator. I didn't know what I would do if I found such a sign. Would I have called the police and given them Carl? Yes, I think I would, but that isn't why I went.

I wanted to verify the story for myself, to see what I was dealing with in Carl.

There was no escalator. I was sure I had the right station. But there was no escalator anywhere in the station. Did Carl mean stairs? If there was no escalator did that mean there was no punch? Was he making the whole thing up? Punching a man to the bottom of an escalator is exactly the kind of thing Carl was capable of and what's more he said he did it. Ultimately I am not convinced it matters, for as I see it Carl could easily have punched a man down an escalator, might as well have punched this man, did punch him.

> Perhaps it never did snow that August in Vermont; perhaps there never were flurries in the night wind, and maybe no-one else felt the ground hardening and summer already dead even as we pretended to bask in it, but that was how it felt to me, and it might as well have snowed, could have snowed, did snow.
>
> *Joan Didion*

Might as well have; could have; did. The movement from possibility to certainty in the sentence is exactly how it works in the head; this is how imagination merges with memory, how dreams get confused with facts; why reality sometimes feels so unreal. The extract is from Joan Didion's *On Keeping a Notebook*. It unlocked my own imagination; something in me resonated strongly and I wanted to use that, the feeling of recognition, almost of ownership, when you read something and think, that's exactly the way *I* feel! And a feeling of entitlement slips in. I started with her line, took some words off, pegged others on – I wanted to absorb the sentence fully, make my own version.

Twenty One

My sister came over this evening, with a nicer than usual bottle of wine.

Look what I found, she said, bringing a tatty cardboard folder out of her bag. Inside the folder was a homemade book called 'Horses and Ponies' that I wrote when I was six. I had forgotten how much my younger self wanted a pony. There are twenty-two pages, hardly any words. Emily insists on holding the book, and pauses at pages that she finds particularly amusing, like the labelled drawings showing the different physical varieties of horse faces:

> Concave
> Convex
> Roman

At first, I am mildly put out at her laughing at me, and I want to hold the book and look at my own pace, but I know, we both know, that we are making up from our quarrel over the lemon tree. Emily laughs hardest at a page of labelled, disembodied legs.

Positions in front

Wide in front
Pigeon-toed
Correct position

Back Positions

Cow hocked
Sickle hocked
Correct position

Twenty Two

I have decided that I should include my own base actions and low words, those that are relevant. I am thinking in particular of something I said to Carl when he was standing on the roof threatening to throw himself off, and something I did while I was trying to break up with him. The material is already so compromised. It has been edited once, by memory, then again by substances – both processes I recognize but can't know the extent of – and now I am editing again, to shape events into a story. I want the story to be true, and I see that if I leave out certain things I said and did, I am taking away from that. This is not to say that I am going back to the attempt to include everything: there has to be some boundaries. But the boundary between the relevant and the irrelevant has moved.

On the roof, he said, I'm ending all of it, and I didn't catch his meaning, so I said, *I've* just ended it, haven't I? No, he said, annoyed, and repeated, with different emphasis: I'm ending *all* of it. I understood, and instantly dismissed, the possibility that he was going to jump to his death. I knew he would not jump. I remember the huge contempt I felt towards him. More than contempt, it was a transforming force. It had fire in it. It contained cruelty. There was a very strong impulse in me and in that moment, I wanted to push him off the roof. Instead, I said something mean. Here are the low words: Go on, then.

His failure to jump made everything worse; I think he felt he had humiliated himself and that seemed to make him angrier. In the long period of unpleasantness afterwards, Carl and I had to go away on business and stay overnight in a hotel. He was angry; this was a tense trip. We had a room with three single beds in it. It was all we could get. He said, I'll sleep in the car. Then he changed his mind. I'm not sleeping in the fucking car; you sleep in the fucking car. Well, I wasn't going to sleep in the car. This was a car we'd fucked in anyway. We went out for dinner; we drove to the restaurant because we were in the middle of nowhere. The meal was appalling, not the food, the tension, he was seething. During the meal, Carl said: I hope whoever you marry beats you and beats your children. There are many things I have forgotten, half remember, misremember, but I remember the exact words and the way his face looked and the way his voice sounded when he uttered this curse. His eyes seemed to darken and shrink, his voice too – he spoke in a harsh whisper – everything retracted into concentrated fury. When he drove back to the hotel, he drove dangerously, on purpose, to scare me. And I was scared. The room was very dark because the hotel was in the countryside. We each got into a single bed, with the spare one between us. Here is the base action: during the night I let him into my bed and had sex with him and the sex was very dark too.

It is quite difficult to write about. Immediately afterwards, Carl punched the wall next to my head, a hard, fast punch, like a continuation of his orgasm – excess passion or aggression he had to shoot into the ground like lightning.

There are other writers I owe a debt. It's not just Joan Didion I have taken from/been inspired by. Absorb, borrow, celebrate, decorate, distort, echo, mirror, pay homage, pay tribute, recycle, rework . . . Steal?

All of these.

Short of outright plagiarism, surely there is a line between inspiration and theft? If the difference is intention, are we talking about conscious or unconscious intent, and where do we draw *that* line?

Sitting on his mother's vast pink bed, Carl played me what he said was her favourite song, 'Only You' by The Platters. I knew the song, and even if I hadn't heard the tune I would have recognized the story, because it is universal: everyone knows it; everyone wants it to be true. Cities have been built and torn down on this myth, wars started, great art created, lives shattered. But I still love the song.

And Carl said, This song is not just my mum's favourite, it's also true, for me, about you: only you can make me feel all right. He said, I feel so alone sometimes, all the time really, just more or less aware of the loneliness: it's not that you make me forget, but when I'm with you, and only when I'm with you, I can know that I'm alone, and not mind. It's better than forgetting. You make it better. Only you.

One night, playing a gig with his band, Carl was drumming so hard and the crowd was so into it that Carl threw his drumsticks out to the crowd and continued to play with his bare hands until someone brought him another set of drumsticks. This aliveness – he just *boomed* – was one of the best things about him.

Carl was convinced that his anger was my fault and, to begin with, I was too. But when he told me about punching the man to the bottom of the escalator, whether that was true or not, I began to see that he was in a state of anger that far exceeded me. He was as sure of this rage as he had been of his love for me. I realized – with a mixture of relief and disappointment – if the anger wasn't all about me then neither was the passion.

I don't know where the line is between passion and obsession but I think obsession is passion that gets stuck.

Perhaps boundaries are like horizons; not fixed, they move as you move, like the end of the rainbow. It's like trying to see when water turns to steam – you can never find that precise moment.

Twenty Three

I have found the most wonderful shop, called Vera's, and there is a real life Vera who runs it. What caught my eye was a dress in the window. On the hanger it looked elegant; dark paisley print, darts, tiny buttons at the wrist, like something Vita Sackville West or Virginia Woolf might have worn, but it looked like a dressing gown on me. (If I ever got another cat I would call her Vita.) Browsing around I found things I need for the flat, but what I like most are the hand written labels: 'Lovely Repro Butter Dish', 'Sweet Little Green "Woods" Jug', 'Two Pretty Vintage Plates', and my favourite – 'Very Old Vermeer Print'.

When I showed Delilah my haul, she rewrote the labels, verbally: 'Was Cheaper First Time Round', 'Bit Of Old Tat', 'Chipped and Faded Plates', 'Fake Grand Master'. She never has seen the charm in secondhand things (unless they're French).

The Vermeer is small and not a terribly good print, which is why it only cost £8.50, but I love it. I have it propped up against the anglepoise lamp on my desk. It's called 'View of

Delft' and shows a line of buildings by a canal, a few tiny people, darkly dressed, but mainly sky and water. I love the faded gold frame, and the proportion of sky, and the soft reflection of the houses on the canal, the way the glass adds reflections of my room into the picture.

After Johnny left, 'our' home did not become 'my' home. The flat looked different because Johnny had taken all his stuff with him and that included pieces of furniture. There were marks on the walls where this furniture had stood for five years, outlines like echoes of the shout I kept hearing in my head: 'HE'S GONE, gone, gone, gone.' Because the rooms were emptier, the walls seemed to stand farther apart than they had before, as if they didn't want to be near me. There was too much space around my clothes in the wardrobe and around my books on the shelf.

I was grateful for Molly's company. She neither approved nor disapproved of me and her evenness was a comfort. After she came back that first time, I began to leave the window open day and night and she came and went as she pleased. I didn't tell Carl, of course. I did away with the litter tray and I never once used the red velvet collar and lead. I buried them in a box of old boots in a cupboard but I didn't dare to throw them out. If I happened to be in the kitchen when Molly made an entrance or exit, I was thrilled, as if by the sighting of a much wilder animal. I loved how she appeared silently on the windowsill and then picked her dainty way onto the counter, and it was wonderful to see her leap from the sill into the garden, wash herself in the sun or run over the dry grass and jump to the top of the wall and disappear over the garage roofs beyond. Her jumps were not jumps, exactly, because they didn't have a start or finish, no obvious effort, they were simply part of her flow.

Molly began to hunt. I found little corpses in the garden, occasionally a dead mouse brought into the house. I didn't know what to do with these – it seemed disrespectful to put them in the bin. Disrespectful to Molly, I mean. Once, I saw her get a bird. I glanced out of the French doors and saw her crouched, taut, the chubby bird twittering about on the grass. Molly crept forward, concentration like a laser fixed her victim to the spot and seemingly had the same effect on me because I did nothing to stop her. She destroyed the bird swiftly using only a fraction of the power I sensed when she was poised on the grass. I was impressed, but I shouldn't have been – cats are predators, predators kill easily. That evening I was in the kitchen, leaning against the counter and eating a bowl of cereal for dinner, Molly came purring, winding herself round me like fabric. I finished the cereal and put the bowl on the counter for Molly to lap the extra milk and as I watched her, I thought, I know you – you are not a kitty.

Seeing Molly discover her own cat-ness gave me another

reason to be angry with Carl for having kept her locked up in that high tower block. It seemed such a strange thing to do. Was he jealous of her? Climbing is quite cat-like and Carl was good at climbing but he was carrying anger and maybe because his anger came from an old wound it didn't seem to fire him but rather to weigh him down. Perhaps that's what bitterness is – old anger. Even the places Carl went to practise – roofs and walls, alleyways between houses – were cat territory.

The other day, sitting here at my desk, I saw a flash of black rush across a rooftop and it made my stomach lurch because I thought of Molly. Of course it was not Molly. It was right at the very edge of my vision so I can't even be sure it was a cat. I haven't seen any cats around here. Probably what I saw was the wing of a crow landing, or taking flight.

> Useless to think you'll park and capture it
> More thoroughly. You are neither here nor there,
> A hurry through which known and strange things pass
> As big soft buffetings come at the car sideways
> And catch the heart off guard and blow it open.
>> *Seamus Heaney*

A memory of Johnny: undressed, lying on our bed after we'd made love one Saturday afternoon, he is looking at raindrops making wobbly tracks down the dirty window, I am lying with my head on his chest, his arm over me, and I am looking up at him, loving him. Why do moments like this pass so quietly? It's not until afterwards that you see them for what they really were; not the times you thought you'd remember, nor the ones you thought you'd miss most, but the ones in which you were truly open. Sometimes, listening to the words of a song or watching a scene in a film, I have a mini epiphany: Oh! I've had moments like that and I didn't realize they were important. It's as though the song or film has framed an episode in your own life so that you see it for the first time, but just as the moment is shown to you, you remember it's already gone.

Sometimes I still wonder: What on Earth made me choose Carl over Johnny? Whatever could it be that brought me to that loss? I bring myself the closest I can to an answer and feel something inside me turn away, to another planet.

I decided to paint the walls white, to cover the marks where Johnny's furniture had been and because I couldn't bear the carnival colours any more. When we first moved in, I wanted bold, rich colours, so I chose a golden yellow for the bedroom, with deep pink woodwork, emerald green walls with pale grey in the sitting room, and kingfisher blue in the kitchen, and then I glossed the whole lot with shiny varnish. It was oppressive, like a funfair when everyone has gone home. Redecorating was a lot of work because I had to do three coats on each wall and all the woodwork, but I embraced it as a penance. The dark brown floors were stripped and sanded and stained white (doing the floors was even more work, so I had someone in to do it – my guilt wasn't bottomless). Around the same time I got new blonde highlights in my hair. I wanted to strip everything away, dip my life in bleach and start new. White walls, blank page – but *tabula rasa* is a myth, of course.

I realize I am confused about beds. I thought that the bed in the dingy hotel where Carl and I first had sex was vast and pink, but I also remember the bed in his mother's room as being vast and pink. Could there be two vast pink beds in this story? I did not have sex with Carl on his mother's bed, but now the notion of Carl's mother and her bed has mingled with the image of Carl and me having sex on that cheap hotel bed; a difficult enough memory on its own, without having his mother mixed up in it.

I remember going into the chief executive's office one day. This woman was a role model for me, so normally I liked going to see her, but I was tired all the time by then, working too hard. She was on the phone when I entered, motioned me to sit and swung her own chair round to face the window as she finished the call. My exhaustion surely affected how I saw things, but all I saw was a grey woman in a grey office on a grey day: grey skin, grey hair, grey suit, grey voice. The sky was the same colour as the walls inside so that it didn't look like outside. At that moment it didn't even seem possible that there was such a thing as outside.

On dull days here, the rooms in the flat opposite are as dark as caves and I think they are empty. Then I see something white and shiny move across a back wall like a thin neon ghost and I can just make out the faint outline of a body underneath. These vests, with the fluorescent strips, are the only protective clothing they wear. They work with their bare hands. I suppose they could be wearing steel toe-capped boots but I have never seen any of them wear a helmet. Today they are working on the roof. They stride nonchalantly across it, attaching hat shaped vent covers. The roof now looks ridiculous, dotted with silly little white hats, but I know I will get used to them and stop seeing them soon enough. If the builders fell they would die. They don't look like they want to die. They look like they believe they are invincible super-heroes. From that height – five storeys, if you count the roof as a level – helmets probably wouldn't be much protection.

Behind them, on a much bigger building site a few streets away, there's an enormous crane. It reaches up into the sky like a giant ladder you could never climb, or part of a huge steel ship. On one side of the crane, at the top of the mast, there is a cabin and a platform, and from the platform, there is a jib, longer than the mast itself. The lifting hook is attached by cables and via wheels and pulleys to the top of the jib. These cables look very heavy. When the crane is lifting they go taut, and when the crane is idle they dip into an elegant curve, which contrasts with all the straight lines and sharp angles.

I can see the man in the cabin. He is always alone up there, in his bubble among the clouds. I imagine that it is the same man every day but I have no way of knowing this because I am not close enough to distinguish any of his features, nor to get an idea of his height or build. I can make out the colours of his clothing. Today, and most days, he is wearing pale blue jeans and a white T-shirt. I can see him put his hand to his head. A lot of the time he just sits there but I can see him if he leans forward or stands up. And I can see his chair, at night, empty.

I convinced myself that I still loved Johnny. We got back together after a small party at my flat. Johnny arrived late, already drunk. He started a fire in the kitchen by spilling a bottle of whiskey and then knocking over a candle so that there was a patch of flames, which scarred the work surface. It was an accident, if you believe in those. Anyway, he stayed late and missed his last train. Johnny and I stayed up drinking and talking until it was light. We passed out in bed together, and later that morning, with terrible hangovers, we made love.

They seem to have an awful lot of breaks over there. Maybe they have to wait for other people to complete things or for deliveries or for things to dry or go hard, maybe, in this way, waiting is part of the job. Sometimes they barely seem to be doing any work at all, and yet visible progress is being made on the flat. More progress than I am making. Often, I will get down a couple of hundred words and then notice a dragging in my stomach that is getting more insistent and I stop, knowing I am veering away from the curve, and by more than a few millimetres. At other times, when I am working well and the builders, or some of them, are also engaged and busy, I feel a sort of companionship-in-work with them.

Johnny once woke me when it was still dark and trundled me over to a window because he thought we could watch the sunrise together; he had got up to go to the toilet and seen a glow on the horizon. We stood there for ages, getting cold, waiting for the dawn. Johnny had his arms around me, mainly to prop me up because I was half asleep. I finally realized what we were watching was not dawn but a fixed light on a crane some distance away. I told him and we went back to bed.

—

I was finding work increasingly stressful; I don't now think it had got any harder, but my ability to cope was dwindling. Often I would find myself dizzy and anxious and I would fear a panic attack or worse, but usually the problem was simply that I had a hangover, had drunk too much coffee and not had enough to eat.

One day, I had been ranting about something and stalked out of the office. I walked around the block and smoked. On the shady side of the pavement, coming towards me, were a mother and small child. The child had a toy puppy on a lead and he and his mother were dawdling along, pretending to walk the puppy. The mother kept glancing up to see if they had been noticed. My anger flooded in. I wanted to kick that puppy clean out of that child's hand, not so much to make the child cry, though that wouldn't have bothered me, but more to rid the mother of her bovine contentedness. The mother's eyes found mine, aren't we adorable, her look said, and oh, the urge was strong, to pitch my sharp toe into the toy and whip it away. The mother quickly looked down; she had seen something deeply wrong in me. I imagined one long strong kick, the kind of kick that would have scored goals, the toy puppy describing a high arc and coming to land in the middle of the hot dusty road with a soft but satisfying *thud*. There is violence in me. I don't know how much.

Twenty Four

This is what it is like to have a secret; it is like hiding a pebble in your fist and having to remember to keep holding it all the time, because if you drop it other people will see and you will be found out. It's like being at the end of a long, satisfying day at the beach, when the whole of you should be spread out to dry in the sun, relaxed and open – but with a secret, there's always one hand clenched. It's lonely. Many affairs must continue way past their natural end because of this loneliness, especially if the two lovers are the only ones who know. If they end the affair, they don't have anyone else to share the secret with.

Confession is not always an impulse towards honesty; telling the truth can be selfish. When I told Johnny about Carl, I thought I was being honest but really I just wanted to unburden myself.

> Above the fresh ruffles of the surf
> Bright striped urchins flay each other with sand.
>
> The sun beats lightning on the waves,

The waves fold thunder on the sand;
And could they hear me I would tell them:

O brilliant kids, frisk with your dog,
Fondle your shells and sticks, bleached
By time and the elements; but there is a line
You must not cross nor ever trust beyond it
Spry cordage of your bodies to caresses
Too lichen-faithful from too wide a breast.
The bottom of the sea is cruel.

Hart Crane

Carl fascinated me because he was new to me. Johnny
had become my standard for what a man was like and it was
a revelation that there were other, saltier, versions of male-
ness. I was interested in everything: the length of his arms,
the breadth of his hands, the depth of his voice. But there
was one early autumn day when we visited a beach together,
the third and last time, and he knew by then that I was
looking past him, at any available horizon, trying, failing,
to make out the difference between the flat grey sea and the
flat grey sky.

We walked along the beach, which was not deserted. I
remember that he was wearing a denim jacket. On the sand,
close to the shoreline, I saw a wallet and bent over to pick it
up. Inside there was a small amount of money, two credit
cards and a card with the owner's name and address. When
I looked up from my find to tell Carl, he was standing a little

way off. I noticed that he was standing weirdly, looking at me. His posture was like a vulture; shoulders hunched over in a tight curl and his head sticking up and out. His face was screwed up in apparent concentration. Then I saw his belt undone and the top of his trousers open, his hand inside, moving fast. I turned and walked quickly away.

My alarm clock broke. Actually it was Johnny's alarm clock, but anyway it broke, and I discovered that it was possible to book an alarm call: you phone a service, tell them what time you want to get up, and your phone rings at that time in the morning and someone, a real person, would say: This is your alarm call, and I would say: Thank you, and then me and the real person would say goodbye to each other, and it was a little bit like having someone there with you to wake you up: a little bit, a tiny little bit, like not being alone.

I left Carl on the beach and travelled home alone to my empty flat, arriving late, and went straight to bed with a bottle of red wine. It was cold. I wore a jumper, scarf and socks and pulled the duvet up to my chest. I drank too much of the wine, and I meant to. I didn't read anything, didn't listen to any music, just sat in bed, drinking, smoking, trying not to think about Carl on the beach but thinking a lot about Carl on the beach and how it had become such a mess with him. The cold white walls reflected the city light. I looked out from my crow's-nest bed at the wooden floorboards and heard the city roar like waves pouring onto a far off shore. And I was adrift, a drunken sailor.

When you booked the alarm call, it was also a real person. But the person you spoke to at night was never the same person who called to wake you in the morning, which was a shame because having spoken to someone just before sleeping it would have been comforting to have the same person wake you. I often got the same night time person, a man. He had a nice voice. I was usually drunk, and he must have heard the alcohol sloshing around my words but he never rushed me when I was prevaricating over a slight variation in my wake up time. I had him for a long stretch – four or five weeks in a row. Foolishly, I felt I was getting to know him. One night I even said to this man that he was becoming a friend.

You don't need a friend. You need an alarm clock, he replied. He didn't sound unkind. In fact, he sounded deeply kind, but embarrassment seared me anyway. Embarrassment and blind, drunken panic, because I didn't know, couldn't think, had absolutely no idea where I could buy an alarm clock.

I don't know where to get one, I said, and hung up.

—

I wrapped up the wallet I found on the beach and posted it back to its owner, with a note explaining where I had found it. A week or so later, I received a letter from the owner. The letter thanked me for returning the wallet with credit cards and money intact and said that the enclosed cheque – for double the sum I had returned – was a reward for my honesty.

After most of my long days at work, I would arrive back at the flat, pour myself a glass of wine or vodka and read, mainly short stories and poetry. I wasn't reading novels because I didn't want that kind of continuity; I didn't want to carry over any part of any narrative from one day to the next. Sometimes I read poetry in languages I didn't fully understand – with a sense of the meaning, but reaching for it, grasping after it. One of my other pleasures was smoking, but I didn't dwell or savour; I narrowed it down to lighting up and the first few drags – after that I lost interest. I read like I smoked: fixating on my new favourite in its entirety to begin with then honing in on the exact phrase or phrases that gave me the fix, then reading only for those, discarding the rest and when that poem had been emptied out, moving on to the next. I liked this line, from Nerval, 'ma seule étoile est morte' (my only star is dead), and this one, from Virgil, 'Sic itur ad astra' (Thus is the way to the stars). I had enough French to work out the line from Nerval, but struggled with the whole poem. I never studied Latin so I can only read it in translation and I have only ever read a few lines of Virgil. Not knowing exactly what the lines mean transforms the words into objects on a shelf, little bottles of amber.

Emily came soon after she heard from Delilah and Shirin. She was brisk. Come on, we'll make a list, she said.

How is a list going to help? It won't solve anything, I said.

Lists are great, very comforting – one thing after another in a nice straight line, said my sister.

> My sister had a gun, and as we walked she would throw bottles into the air and shoot as many as she could before they hit the ground. I had nothing but to walk into nowhere and the wide sunset space with the star.
>
> *Georgia O'Keefe*

I thought that writing a list in this situation was like trying to catch a storm in a butterfly net – this must have been only a few weeks before Carl's death and though nobody guessed that this was what was coming, the feel of something dreadful was hanging, low, in the air. Undaunted by the threatening weather, my sister set to work like the fairy godmother arriving just after the wicked fairy has cast her spell; she can't undo the magic, but she can soften it a little.

She looked in the fridge and tutted. She listed the days of the week and against each day she wrote what I would have for breakfast, lunch and dinner, which we consulted on, and then this list branched into a detailed shopping list, and she summoned Harry, her smooth new man, to come along in his sleek black colt of a car and charged him with the shopping, which he did, generously adding some ideas of his own, mainly chocolate but also one bottle of very good red wine, which was brave of him because I think he had been instructed to omit alcohol. Harry delivered the shopping discreetly, and left, which, had I been paying any heed, was a clue to how serious things were, or how seriously my sister and friends were taking things.

My sister made calls because she didn't think I should be alone. Johnny was included, because we were back together at this point, although he was still living in the yellow room at Robbie's. I made a disparaging remark about the baby-sitting circle but my sister was not to be dissuaded and the list lengthened, itemizing who would be with me on each evening.

> Mon: Johnny and Emily
> Tue: Shirin
> Wed: Johnny
> Thur: Emily and Delilah
> Fri: Delilah and Shirin
> Sat: Emily
> Sun: Shirin and Johnny

Making the lists did create a sense of order, something that I could hold on to, at least for a few days. My sister had spun me a silken ladder. Such showmanship! It reminds me now of the Indian test for cashmere: if the cashmere is of the finest quality – as soft and light as a cloud – then a large shawl will pass easily through a woman's wedding ring.

> It needs a good woman, or a good girl will do, to bring you back from the stony desert that runs up flat to a precipice where the soul hangs by a thread over the abyss. And what is down below? Hell. And don't say you don't believe in hell or hell may get the laugh of you. And hanging by a sisal twist over the darkling void lit by an electric blue flash, like mending the tram lines, you know that blue flash?
>
> *Stevie Smith*

Next my sister had a good hard look at my flat, still empty since Johnny had removed his things and I had not yet replaced any of them, and made a list of what was needed, which included stuff like cushions and rugs, blankets and lamps, and then she called upon Shirin and Delilah, who appeared with quilts and pillows and scented candles. Delilah brought a large round rug from her own home and Shirin brought several floor cushions that used to be on her family's roof terrace in Tehran. The three of them prepared food, turned off the lights and lit candles, played gentle music, and all the soft sounds and low light and cooking smells transformed my flat into a place with fewer hard corners. I didn't have a table so we sat on the floor and ate soup and rice and syrup pudding. No wine, that night, which is probably why I remember it so well. Also I remember it because of the luxury of being looked after, which I hadn't had since very young. When we were little girls, my sister and I visited our grandmother together and she would indulge us: I liked mushroom soup, my sister preferred tomato; I liked chocolate cake, she liked Victoria sponge; I liked fried eggs, she liked boiled, that kind of thing. Alongside the comfort was this sense of being helped.

> At times I have the feeling someone else is working on this with me. I read a passage I haven't looked at in weeks and I don't recognise much of it, or only dimly, and I say to myself, Well, that's not bad, it's a reasonable solution to *that* problem. But I can't quite believe I was the one who found the solution. I don't remember finding it, and I am relieved, as though I expected the problem still to be there.
>
> *Lydia Davis*

I looked at the list on Wednesday morning.

Wed: Johnny

And I suddenly knew without any doubt that I would not wed Johnny. I didn't know why; I just knew that I didn't want to. Our reunion had only lasted a couple of months; luckily he hadn't moved back in so splitting up with him the second time was easier and quicker. And so, making the lists, did, in fact, solve something important.

'View of Delft' makes me feel spacious, gives working a dreamy quality – I am less craven, less inclined to muscle through. I still want precision but the way I go about reaching it is softer.

Sometimes I just leave it, go onto the terrace to see the courtyard garden, water my plants, or go for a walk along the canal, which is only ten minutes away. Of course the light is never the same as in the Vermeer and it's more industrial, but I like looking at the houseboats and I like walking beside water.

Before they could get out of Iran, Shirin's father was arrested and put in prison for five months. Shirin and her mother and sisters prepared for the inevitable raid on their house. There was a collection of fine glass animals, each a different colour, each full of alcohol, which had to be destroyed. They smashed them in the bath. Shirin described the stench of spirits, the stickiness of the liqueurs, the bottom of the bath covered with broken glass.

Now she collects sea glass, mainly green, some bright blue, some dark brown, and some white pebbles that used to be bits of clear glass until they were scratched and soothed by sand and water over many years and made opaque. She'll hold them under a running tap to show me how the colour changes in water. She keeps the glass in a wooden box with a metal clasp and brings it out in handfuls to make a pile of riches on the table. One day she plans to make a mosaic but when she spreads out her collection with her hand across the table, it seems to me a work of art already.

I see now that much of the heightened emotion during and after the affair came from me, but not all of it. Other people noticed Carl's behaviour towards me. One evening at work, one of Carl's mates came over to talk to me. He sat on Carl's desk in a casual manner, dangling his legs, and he told me that he and the rest of Carl's team knew what Carl was doing – making threats, intimidating me – but that they couldn't stop him. Cowards, I thought. Even Carl's friends were frightened of him; and he wasn't threatening *them*.

One day not long before he was sacked, he and I had a meeting. We used an empty office on the same floor as the rest of our division. We could have used the meeting room upstairs but I remember thinking that was too far away from other people. We were sitting at a hexagonal table, opposite each other. The door was closed. Carl sat silent, glaring at me. He couldn't contain himself for long. Something I said angered him. He stood up, muttered something thick and toxic, and then raised his arm and brought his fist down, punching the table hard. The door opened and a colleague, Sara, came in.

Is everything OK in here? I heard a bang. I thought maybe a filing cabinet had fallen over or something, Sara said.

We all knew that she didn't think the noise had been a filing cabinet. Carl walked out of the room.

The next day he sheepishly told me that he had been to the hospital for an X-ray and had cracked a bone in his hand. He was mild that morning, he even made me a cup of tea, but the situation felt dangerous and out of control. After Carl's death, a policewoman told me that Carl hitting the table, and the steering wheel, and the door, and the wing mirror, and the wall, was the next best thing to hitting me. I have held on to this as a defence.

Carl found a new girlfriend. The main thing I remember about her was that she was very young. Too young to know what suited her – she wore her thick blonde hair in a helmet shaped bob – but young enough that it didn't matter. She was about five years younger than me, and at least ten years younger than Carl. Her name was Michelle, or Sheryl. He brought her into work a few times, to show her off, to show everyone that he hadn't totally lost it, but mainly to show me. Remembering it this way is revealing, perhaps because I have to admit some difficult feelings. I should have been relieved that Carl had someone else, but I resented being replaced so easily. Having a new girl didn't stop Carl being vicious to me, so I realized fairly quickly that I had not, actually, been replaced and I was smug about that, which put me in the position of almost welcoming his harassment. I was all twisted up.

I saw a note on Carl's desk one night when I was working late. I knew it was from Sheryl/Michelle. The note was folded, not sealed, so I read it. The message was innocuous; an expression of affection, I think, but I clearly remember her handwriting, fat round letters barely joined up, like a baby's limbs. Her handwriting made me feel guilty because it showed me her innocence, and at the same time I knew I was prepared to sacrifice her, prepared to see her consumed in the flames of whatever happened between Carl and me. I was not sisterly to that girl.

The morning they sacked him, our director called me into his office to tell me first. When I came back to my desk, Carl threw me a look so cold and mean that I was afraid of what he might do next. He knew what was going to happen and calmly cleared his desk, packing his personal things into his little rucksack. He did this slowly, perhaps to show that he wasn't intimidated by having to go and see the director and the chief executive to be told to leave the building for good. Or maybe he was trying to intimidate me by taking his time. His final gesture that morning, after collecting his things and turning off his computer, was to take his bunch of keys out of his jacket pocket, separate off the office keys and lay them on his desk.

I assumed he hated me even more because he was losing his job over me, but now I think he was frustrated because he would lose his chance to carry on punishing me. He seemed to hate me so much by then that it may have been preferable to feed his anger by being near me than to be away from me and have to find other ways to sustain the rage.

He put on his jacket, put his rucksack over one shoulder and said goodbye to my assistant, shaking his hand. He was only trying to retain some dignity but I remember a surge of irritation, Get on with it, I wanted to say. He wasn't being sent to the gallows after all.

— Have you made any plans?
— Take an overdose, slash my wrists then hang myself.
— All those things together?
— It couldn't possibly be misconstrued as a cry for help.
Sarah Kane

Twenty Five

I haven't done any writing for a week. Something has changed underneath me like a tide. (Maybe this hasn't just happened in the last few days, maybe it started before and has only just surfaced.) It reminds me of when I gave up smoking, five years ago. I thought it would be difficult – it's supposed to be – but in fact it was simple: I just realized that my position had changed. I found that I wanted to not smoke more than I wanted each individual cigarette.

> I do not any longer feel inclined to doff the cap to death. I like to go out of the room talking, with an unfinished casual sentence on my lips.
>
> *Virginia Woolf*

A memory from the hospital: I remember being pleased because I had a good spot in the corner of the ward. I thought, I am lucky: I have two walls, nobody gets four walls and most have none. The woman next to me had no walls, only curtains. I heard a doctor ask her if she had ever had an operation. She told the doctor she had had her spleen out. Her ex ruptured it. Now she had to get her remaining, splintered teeth removed. Did he rupture those too?

You have to work it out for yourself. Sometimes it is difficult to see the point in even trying, but mostly I do see it, and the point is to be free (technically I *am* free, but this could be reversed). I recall the increasing claustrophobia of that time, how it felt like being in a coffee press, plunging steadily down and down, less and less room to breathe. Starless. The hole behind your life can't be filled with sorrows or cigarette smoke. And my argument with myself – why did I go on, why did I stay, why did I leave . . . I can never win and it doesn't fill the hole. It's just a habit.

I used to think that weeding and watering plants would be chores like dusting or ironing, neither of which I do, but there's not much weeding and actually I like watering – it's quite restful. The plants are doing OK – the lemons are nowhere near yellow and it's nearly the end of August, but at least they are still on the tree.

Earlier, two of the builders were cutting through red brick on the side of the building. The tool they used was loud and high-pitched but more distracting was the cloud they created – billows of rosy dust that looked lovely from where I sit, though surely not lovely to be in. Now it is very hot and these two are stretched out and inert on the roof like a pair of lizards.

I don't actually lie out in the sun – too many men around – but daydreaming feels a bit like sunbathing. My wall is sandy coloured and if it is hot, then by noon the sun has made the bricks golden and inviting and I want to feel their heat on my hand, arm, shoulder, cheek – and stay for a moment, resting against the warm wall.

Twenty Six

I have said I had a breakdown after Carl's death, but I don't like saying it. I prefer the word 'crisis', although that sounds too quick because whatever happened went on for months and in the middle of that I was in the hospital for weeks.

The doctors gave me a sedative that warped my mental processes, though my mind was already strained to the maximum, memory already ragged. The pills made everything I did very slow, both physically and in my head, but they didn't give me the rest I was longing for. One hundred enchanted years would have been lovely. All I wanted was to be soaked in sleep, to wake up drenched in it, but I would wake in the night, needing to pee, viciously thirsty, internal organs exhausted, especially liver and lungs, from processing alcohol and caffeine and tobacco, and now these pills.

Perhaps I had a breakdown because I wanted to run away. I ploughed a lot of effort into that breakdown, though I didn't know that's what I was doing. At least, I didn't know at the top of my head. Somewhere underneath I might have known.

During Carl's ranting and raging I existed in a state of perpetual alert. I bought a pocket alarm, in fact it was a rape alarm. I was afraid he might follow me and intimidate me in some way. There was a short path leading from my front door to the pavement and a patch of dry, bare mud that could have been a small front garden but wasn't because of the shadow cast by an enormously tall, thick, brambly hedge that scratched skin, pulled hair and tore clothing. I suppose the hedge was my responsibility to maintain, but I never did anything about it and neither did the people who lived upstairs so it grew and grew and grew until pedestrians began to cross to the other side of the road because it took up all the pavement. There was a narrow corridor between the hedge and my bedroom window and my main fear was that Carl would be hiding in this space, waiting for me when I got home.

I developed a habit of calling the police. It was an escalation of the alarm calls habit, which I hadn't quit. Any time I sniffed violence, I called. Walking along a street I came upon a man and a woman, he was walking ahead issuing threats and she was following behind, pleading. He had obviously beaten her before, and he was obviously going to do it again, and so I called the police. Another time, I heard a fight in the road outside my flat. It was late at night and I could hear male voices shouting and punches landing, and so I called the police, but the fight stopped and the men went away of their own accord. Even though the police came, each time, I kept calling them because I didn't feel answered. And perhaps I also sensed that they would be needed soon, for real.

The builders are bored today. Two of them are jousting with long cardboard tubes, I can see them through the two lower windows, dancing back and forth across the floor. I wanted Johnny to be my knight in shining armour, my champion, my dragon slayer, my avenging prince on a charging white steed, which was probably why I got back together with him.

In the hospital, each bed had a curtain that could be drawn right around, a parody of a four-poster bed, and the curtain design was a repeating pattern of blue crowns in diagonal rows. I clearly remember the sound of the metal curtain rings on the metal rail whenever the brisk nurses pulled the curtains; like the rush of small, heavy coins being emptied from a velvet purse onto a long table, or the crunching of chainmail on the arm that picks them up.

—

The woman who runs the Spanish restaurant owns the whole of the building opposite and she is in the flat, viewing progress. The builders are moving around more than usual, looking busy. I know this woman because I go to her restaurant quite often now. She glances over into my room and sees me sitting at my desk, but she looks away again as if she hasn't seen me. Whenever we see each other at ground level, we say hello. I don't think she is being rude today. I think it's just that up here there is a different etiquette. She is respecting my privacy, but this privacy doesn't actually exist, as the builders, and me – and my sister – all well know. And yet I do not relieve her of this charade, I do not call Hello! or wave. She prefers to think I retain some privacy and I prefer to let her think that.

The police had a lot of questions for me after Carl's death. Every day the doctors brought the police to my bedside. They came to ask their questions, drawing the royal curtain, arranging themselves in a horseshoe around the foot of the narrow metal bed and each time they came all I could think, my only thought was, Will this horseshoe hold my luck, or will it all run out? Their questions came fast and sharp, knives thrown at a target. My instinct was to protect myself and this is why I didn't speak. My silence allowed me to listen, and what I heard was that they really only had one question. How doggedly they asked this question. And how furiously they wanted an answer.

I wanted to answer, but with what? It was in the hospital that I first started to write it down. It was Shirin's idea: If you can't talk about it, why don't you try writing down what happened? Remember, remember and write it down. I started to record what I could remember, vaguely aware of this thing nudging at me that wanted to be fed or watered or let out. And the next day, when they came and drew the curtain and stood in a horseshoe at the end of the narrow metal bed and asked me their questions, I was able to answer, I'm writing it down. They were not entirely satisfied, but one of them persuaded the others to leave me alone, saying, She's writing it down. As they walked away I thought, My luck is holding.

The only things in my fridge were coffee and vodka. I never ran out of coffee or vodka. Occasionally I would buy fruit, intending to eat an apple a day, but often the skin would go wrinkly and the flesh would shrink, and I wouldn't notice until the apples were actually disintegrating, and then I would throw them out and, a few days later buy fresh apples to lie innocently in the bowl, untouched, until they too started to rot.

One morning I picked a new apple from the bowl to take

to work, red on one side, green on the other, shiny, firm; a perfect Disney apple. Later that day, sitting at my desk, I took a bite. The apple was too big and too sweet. I noticed the sweetness of it hanging on my lips and inside my mouth and I had to wash the taste away with a gulp of water. I set it aside. The apple lay on the windowsill, gradually browning where I had bitten it.

When I noticed it again I became annoyed with myself: until the affair with Carl I had been a hearty eater but now I was a pathetic creature who couldn't manage a whole apple. Who the hell did I think I was – Snow White, choking on the red skin of the poisoned apple? Except that I didn't require a wicked stepmother to poison me, I was doing the job myself with drink and cigarettes.

> Everywhere there were people living out their lives using aspects of suicide against themselves. They did not even have the authenticity of the final act to speak for them. Suicide is, in short, the one continuous, every-day, ever-present problem of living. It is a question of degree.
>
> *Daniel Stern*

When Shirin visited me in hospital she would tell me stories about being a little girl in Tehran, and what it was like having to leave Iran aged eleven and finish her childhood in another country; she had to learn how to be Iranian in England, which is an entirely different thing to being

Iranian in Iran. There was so much that she had to relearn — reprogram, actually — in order to fit in. For example, when she fell, she was used to saying, 'Ai!' but she learned to say, 'Ow!' instead. Even the shortest utterances that one assumes to be instinctual aren't; they are learned behaviour.

The day the Shah left Iran, she smoked her first cigarette. That night there was a gathering at her parents' house and when the adults went to dinner, Shirin who was ten years old and her friend Ali who was eight rifled through all the bags looking for cigarettes and took a single one from every packet they found. Upstairs, in her bathroom, they compared their loot.

I got a Winston!

I got a Marlboro!

I got a Silvester!

I got a Dunhill!

They smoked standing over the sink, coughing their guts out. When, later, the adults challenged the children, they flat denied it.

I read that we start growing up with the first lie we tell our parent figure, so it follows that when you carry out a crime, or a misdemeanour, and don't confess; that's grown up.

I tried to run away through work and other drugs. Even when I was with him, work served as a welcome distraction from Carl, and afterwards I used it even harder. Maybe I thought I could make up for everything I had done wrong by being good at work. Maybe I thought long hours in the office could ground me. Or that if I did well in my job, somehow this would balance out the lies I had told, like there was some kind of Virtue/Sin balance sheet and someone was keeping score. But I wasn't at the front of my face. Even though I was physically present at work, much of the time I would sit in my chair, staring out of the window, feeling around in my hairline, touching my spots as if they were little ornaments, dusting them with my fingers.

Returning from work in the evenings, everyone around me looked tired and loose and drab, and all I could see was beaten down men and women with droopy shoulders in bad suits and cheap shoes. And trees with branches outstretched waiting for the day to drop into their arms, exhausted.

At home, after feeding Molly, I liked to pour myself a glass of wine or vodka, sit on the rough wooden steps to the garden with the light of the kitchen behind me, light a cigarette – a Marlboro Light, preferably a soft pack – and read poetry, especially, then, John Keats. I liked the voluptuousness of Keats on death.

I was hooked. Not just on the drinking, the smoking, the reading of poetry, but on the idea of myself drinking and smoking and reading poetry. I stood apart from myself and watched. I had to reach the point where I could pass out as soon as I tipped into bed, but it was difficult to judge. Sometimes I drank and smoked until I could barely stand up to brush my teeth and sometimes I would wake to find myself on the sofa with the lights still on and drool on my shoulder. A pattern emerged: every night I would work late, until half-past nine when it was dark or even later, and then go home and drink and smoke until I simply cut out, and every morning, coming round after a night of inadequate sleep, with a furry mouth and a fuzzy mind, I would light the first cigarette, bitter, necessary, and brew the coffee strong and hot: the black coffee and the dry cigarette working to cut through the fog from the night before. And that was my life. Evenings: cutting out. Mornings: cutting through.

Twenty Seven

I wanted to love Johnny. I thought that I might fall in love with him again. He had not yet fallen out of love with me and he was willing to forgive me, I think, but only if I worked. This was an unspoken condition. Perhaps he noted how hard I was working in my paid job and thought that I should be putting an equal if not greater amount of effort into repairing our relationship. He had no way of knowing that even though I was putting the hours in at the office, I spent a lot of time staring into space and picking spots, and that the effort I was making at work was much less than it seemed. By the time Johnny and I got back together, Carl had been sacked and this also met a condition for Johnny; he could not have tolerated me spending each working day in the vicinity of my ex-lover. Before we got together again, Johnny slept with a woman he met at a conference. He didn't tell me; I just knew. I don't know how I knew, but I did. Perhaps I smelt it. When I asked him about her the only thing he would say was that she was petite, which made me feel lumpy. Although I didn't like the thought of him with another woman, I could hardly complain. And anyway, having slept with someone else was another condition for Johnny.

Falling in or out of love – what does that mean, exactly? How long does it take to fall in love? Thirty seconds? One minute? A minute's fall is a long, long way down. There is no hope of survival. Fallen in love is like fallen in battle – dead and gone. Sometimes people say, 'I was falling in love with her/him, but . . . ' This 'but' is curious; it implies that they stopped falling, but how? Dropping onto a ledge? Grabbing a convenient branch on the way down like they do in cartoons? Opening a parachute? No. It's not like that. The whole idea of 'falling' in love is wrong. One doesn't 'fall' in love; one simply *knows*. You know in an instant whether or not you could love a person. There is an opening towards that person, a sense of coming forward, of discovery.

I'll be watching the crane – mesmerized – looking up at the man in the clouds and then realize the builders are watching me so I come back to my work and my desk where my anglepoise lamp is a scaled-down version of the crane, minus the man. I want to wave at him, partly to discover if he can see me from such a height and distance, but if I do that, the builders might think I am waving at them.

—

I wondered why I couldn't make myself do what I should to mend it with Johnny. I just knew that trying made me sad and tired.

You are not working hard enough on this relationship, he said, and it was true but by saying this he squeezed the ambivalence out of me, like getting rid of a pocket of air – the trouble is, I was breathing that air.

There are no builders in sight. I attempt a wave at the crane driver but just as I lift my arm and start waving one of the builders, the fat-faced one, comes to the window. I abort the wave soon enough that he couldn't possibly think I was waving at *him*, but unfortunately it did attract his attention. It's pointless anyway, waving at the man in the crane because if we met in the street we wouldn't recognize each other. He may as well be the man in the moon.

It is said that you are not over the last lover completely until you are into the next one. Johnny must have heard this too because when we split up for the second time, he found a new girlfriend almost immediately and he was already quite established with her by the time Carl died. The weird thing was that she was also called Rachel. Of course I quizzed him. How did they meet? How old was she? What did she do? Where did she live? And, most importantly: what did she look like? He told me all, enjoyed it rather, I thought, and fair enough. He said she was beautiful 'in a classical way' but he didn't give me enough to go on: I couldn't *see* her. Classical how, exactly? I asked. Like a Greek goddess? A Roman coin?

What I really wanted to ask (but didn't) was, Am I prettier than?

I would wake early, often around 5 a.m. One morning I pushed my feet into some old trainers, pulled on a cardigan and went out to the shop looking for cigarettes. It was already light and birds were singing but the streets were empty apart from an old drunk shouting at the sky; just another person wrestling with his demons. Along came a young businessman in a suit striding down the pavement. I asked him if he had a light, but I must have startled him because he drew back as if I had scorched him and then walked around, giving me a wide berth. This man would have seen me as a peer at 9 a.m. but at 5 a.m., he clearly didn't. I was puzzled by this at first and then realized what I must have looked like to him: snaggly unwashed and un-brushed hair, old pyjama bottoms, skanky trainers, bags under my eyes, tired skin – I probably looked more like the old drunk's daughter than a young professional. Instead of seeing this as a warning sign, I was filled with contempt: my pyjamas may have been old but they were *satin*, for goodness' sake, and that fool didn't recognize a princess when he saw one.

We think we can escape down half-deserted streets but all the things we use to defend ourselves – overworking, over-drinking, over-eating, under-eating, smoking, etc. – are well-worn pathways. The really frightening thing about the abyss is not that it exists, but that there is always a road in, and we take it.

The fat-faced builder keeps popping up at the window, usually with a phone pressed to his ear. He may have good reason to be on the phone, perhaps he's the foreman or something, but there are other places he could talk, it doesn't have to be the window opposite me. I think the phone is an alibi.

(Usually I object to the use of the word 'pop' unless it refers to bread in the toaster, or bubbles. I can't stand it when people say they are going to 'pop' to a shop, for example. Toast pops. Bubbles pop. People do not. And yet I can't think of a better way of describing how the fat-faced builder appears at the window; he really does pop up – like a Jack-in-the-box. Or toast.)

Twenty Eight

The bottle of whiskey on Carl's desk was the excuse they finally used to sack him. I don't know where the whiskey came from. I have a feeling that Sheryl/Michelle gave it to him, though she could barely have been old enough to purchase alcohol. In any case, the whiskey was important to him. It sat on his desk, an open gesture of defiance. The bottle had been opened, some of the whiskey had been drunk, but the level never seemed to go down. And yet Carl would arrive, late, unwashed and unshaven for days at a time, with puffed shadows under his eyes. He wouldn't make eye contact. He was definitely drinking something hard, but not from this bottle.

The whiskey reminded me of the perfume that Carl gave me at the very beginning of our affair: same square bottle only larger, our affair book-ended by these two bottles of amber liquid, with the end much bigger than the beginning. Like the perfume on my shelf, which signalled Carl's entry into my life, the whiskey on his desk became largely symbolic, something to do with his exit. He was sacked for a symbolic reason, and he accepted that. I see now there was a certain dignity in how he played that.

I was slowly merging back in with my people – management, the rule-makers – and as I re-joined my group, he struck out on his own. Without a job, or some sort of structure to undermine, what does a rule-breaker do? Carl had more time for brooding. Perhaps he also spent a lot of time at the climbing wall, or climbing random buildings, I don't know, but certainly his obsession darkened and deepened. I used to think that I was the object of his obsession but now I am not so sure that obsession *has* an object – I think there are vehicles that the obsessive locks onto, thinking they will carry the weight of it, take some of the unbearable heavy pain away, but of course they don't – can't, even if they are willing to.

Last night I was woken by horrible shrill screams that went on and on. They came from the street outside. When I looked out of the window I saw a fox in the street. Perhaps it had been chasing or fighting something but now it stood silent by a parked car, looking down the dark street, and then leapt onto a high wall and padded softly away. I was surprised how small and thin it was – not much bigger than an adult cat – and how nimble. This morning I saw muddy paw prints on the skylight in my room, I wondered if they were made by the fox, but I didn't hear anything on my roof last night. I suppose they could have been there before and I just didn't notice them. I can't tell by the size of the paw prints if they belong to a fox or a cat. Now it is raining heavily and they are being washed away.

The crane is like a weather vane for a different stratum: when idle, the lifting hook hangs so very high that it sways even when the air is breathless down here. I like to watch the crane turn sedately and I like to see what comes up on the hook (earlier it was a great bundle of dripping blue net that looked like it had been dredged up from the bottom of the sea). Often the crane doesn't move at all for quite long periods of time and the man waits alone up there in his bubble.

Today he's wearing blue jeans and a red T-shirt. At the moment he is out of sight because the cab has swung right round. Then back he slowly comes, with tons of blocks wrapped in a blue plastic sheet that flutters in the breeze like washing on a line. I am beginning to understand why people watch sports like cricket or darts or golf.

There seems to be much more traffic in the sky. Or maybe I am simply seeing what is already there because I am looking at the crane so much.

Twenty Nine

I didn't want to let Molly go, especially to this crazed freak, but I wanted the calls and threats to stop and she was, after all, his. He wanted his cat back. He had just moved into a flat on the fifth floor. A friend of his at work gave me the address and a key. The plan was that I would take Molly and all her things to this flat. Carl would be out. I wanted to see Molly into her new home, and maybe I was curious as to what sort of life that would be, what sort of place Carl was in now.

The morning I was due to deliver Molly, I dug out her lead from the dusty box and took my shoes out of her cat basket. I washed the red and white gingham cushion by hand, cleaned the food and water bowls, and wiped the inside of the basket with a hot cloth. The litter tray had long gone and I had asked Carl via his friend to buy a new one. I folded over the top of the bag of cat food and sealed in its pungent, salty smell with tape. I had bought some single cream for Molly, as a treat, and imagined basking in the sun with her or having her paddle my lap and then sleep on me for one last time, but of course that didn't happen – it was a grey day and Molly was nowhere to be seen. This made me anxious and I began thinking I should have kept her in the night before. But she's going to be a prisoner again soon enough, I thought, damning Carl for choosing a high rise flat. Anyway. Molly came back and the taxi came. There wasn't time to give Molly the cream.

I carried her and all her things up five flights of stairs and didn't stop until I got to the door – blue, with a frayed, dusty doormat and some take-away menus and a free local newspaper sticking out of the letterbox. I reached into my back pocket for the key and went in. I wasn't sure how to say goodbye. I was sweating and out of breath and now I started to cry. The flat was horrible, as I knew it would be. Molly jumped down from my shoulder. Her weight leaving mine was a physical wrench. I suppressed the tears; the journey here had taken longer because of traffic and Carl would be back soon. No time for crying. A state-of-the-art television dominated the room, a huge thing, silver, like my car.

So much of it happened in cars. With Carl, the parallel lines arrangement of driving soon suited me; sitting next to someone in a car does not require intimacy. When things were bad between us, in the period when I was trying to break up with him but before I really had, we barely spoke for a four-hour journey. I was driving. It was dark. I was thirsty. A small bottle of water lay at his feet, I kept looking at it, wondering if I could lean down and reach it myself but

I was scared to in case he kicked me. He probably wouldn't have kicked me, but that is how the atmosphere was. As we approached the outskirts of the city, I broke the silence: Could I have a drink of water?

You want a drink of water?

Yes, please, I said.

Right.

Carl wound down the passenger window and threw the bottle out. He wound the window back up. He didn't say anything else, and neither did I.

Carl's apartment – Molly's new home – was filled with stale air. There was a full ashtray on the floor beside the big television and a few empty beer bottles. The gingham cushion that went inside Molly's basket was still damp; it would absorb the smell thoroughly and I chided myself for not having made time to dry it in my garden. There was nothing green or alive in this place and from this side of the room, not even a tree was visible. I went to the sash window and opened it as far as it would go. It slid up easily and banged at the top. There was a pedestrian square immediately below, some bushes and litterbins around it and, a street or two away, the tops of trees swaying in the breeze. I looked for the highest leaf, which took some time because the branches were moving, found it and then realized how much it bothered me that I couldn't see the trunks of these trees: This is all wrong,

I thought – to keep a cat in a room higher than the trees she should be climbing – it's all upside down.

I folded up the plastic carrier bag and put it next to the basket. I would have to say goodbye now. The last clear thing I remember from that afternoon is the sharp relief with which I noticed her empty water bowl: I couldn't leave her without water! I took the bowl into the kitchen to fill. When I came back into the sitting room, with the full bowl of water, Molly was crouching on the windowsill, looking out of the open window, attentive. Misgiving shot through me but it was too late. A bird flew past; she leapt.

Yesterday evening I went out and, at the end of my street, by the church, I walked through the smell of a fox. There was a definite edge to it – I walked in and out of it a few times, to check – and then tried to pinpoint the source; I went up close to some shrubbery by the church door but it only smelt of greenery, and so I put my nose to the walls and they only smelt of brick and dust. I couldn't locate the smell on something concrete (I wasn't going to get down and sniff the pavement) and yet it was such a strong presence, hanging in the air like an invisible cloud.

I don't remember what I did with the water bowl. I don't remember getting out of the flat and down the stairs and out onto the concrete where Molly lay. There was no need to check whether she had survived the drop and yet there was no blood, at least I don't remember any. I don't think I touched her. I have no idea how long I knelt by her side. I don't remember Carl showing up; he was suddenly there. Words may have been spoken, but not many were necessary. It was obviously an accident; animals don't commit suicide, although another way of looking at it is that I gave Molly a way out and she took it. Carl dropped down and placed both his hands very gently on Molly's soft body. His own body juddered with soundless sobbing. We were kneeling together like this, for a moment. Then something shifted – I am almost certain that my fear took hold just before his anger arrived and that I got to my feet before he lunged at me, otherwise I don't know how I would have got away from him. I ran into the apartment block, up five flights of stairs, back into the flat and slammed the door shut. Carl was behind me for some of it, I heard his footsteps landing heavy on the staircase and heard him curse me, but by the time I shut the door he was not there. I cut my hand on the latch when I locked the door behind me, so now there was my blood, none of Molly's and none, yet, of Carl's. Strange that mine should be the first blood on the floor. I held the bleeding hand with the other hand but I couldn't feel the cut. I was shaking hard now; fear and adrenalin chased the breath out of my body and it felt like drowning.

—

I saw a painting by Jasper Johns in the New York Museum of Modern Art, or it might have been the Met. The painting is called 'Diver' and is about the death of the poet Hart Crane, who committed suicide by jumping off the back of a boat into the Gulf of Mexico, off the Florida coast. I hadn't known this about Hart Crane until I saw the painting. As I remembered it, the painting featured his two dark brown footprints on a dark red background, but when I looked it up again recently it wasn't like that at all – it's more watery. I actually prefer the version I have in my head to the real painting but anyhow, it shows Hart Crane's dive, as a suspended moment between life and death; just a moment between the two. I think that's terrifying, and a little bit thrilling. It reminds me of Johnny telling me to let myself fall into the pool below the waterfall.

I would have been better off running away from Carl in the streets. Running into his building and up to his apartment and slamming the door was like running away from him by running towards him.

The time I locked the office door after Carl without thinking not only kept him away from me but also stopped me from going after him. This time was different. On neither occasion was reasoning involved and yet both times a choice was made, my body decided and my head wondered about my real intention afterwards.

—

Apparently I called the police from Carl's flat. They have my name and the time of the call on record and have shown me this and yet I have no memory whatsoever of speaking to them. Apparently I said that Molly was dead and that Carl was coming to get me. I didn't mention that Molly was a cat, which would be another reason they came so quickly. The fact that I called the police helped me later; it cast me more as a victim than a perpetrator.

Thirty

At Carl's funeral, I begin to cry and as I do, I realize that I haven't yet done so, about Carl or about Johnny, which only seems like another failure and so I cry all the way through the funeral. I am genuinely crying but I am also aware that this looks good, or better than being completely dry-eyed, especially since the two police officers who were first on the scene attend the funeral. The detectives who visited and questioned me in hospital were not present, but I figured that the two police officers would tell the two detectives that I was inconsolable.

Our Kid wore a black suit, which he managed to make look like a pair of pyjamas, just the way they hung, loosely, off him. Perhaps he made everything he wore look like pyjamas, or perhaps it wasn't his suit. Our Kid was forlorn. I couldn't help feeling that he had been orphaned again by Carl's death and I cried about this too. My sister, who accompanied me and looked incredible in a tight black dress and hair in a sober ponytail, said: It's not your responsibility, *he's* not your responsibility. But he has *nobody*, I wept.

Well then, who's that? she riposted, gesturing to a portly older woman sitting next to Our Kid. An *aunt*, I wailed. Aunts are great, said my sister crisply, and we left.

My sister came to stay after Carl was killed, but I didn't want a nursemaid. What I wanted was not to have been there and since this could not be achieved I set out to de-wire that part of my brain so I literally couldn't go there again.

> I do not want to read, draw, talk or see tonight. I hope this doesn't last long.
>
> *Francesca Woodman*

I felt dizzy and sick the whole time; I was in a constant free-fall. I knew, intuitively, that when I hit the ground it was going to be bad because I was falling so far but after several days I was willing that hard landing because I just wanted to stop spinning. It wasn't enough to kill the thought. And so, when my sister was out for the night, I took some pills.

It was like the nursery rhyme about the old lady who swallowed a fly: I took the pills to swallow the drink, I took the drink to swallow the smoke, I took the smoke to swallow the caffeine, I took the caffeine to swallow the thought that wrangled and jangled and chewed my insides. Chiefly what I remember of the overdose – although you can't really call it remembering, it's more an impression – is a sense of merging, no separation anywhere. Know. Don't know. And then forget. Swim on, strong strokes, go deeper, until the river gives into the deep green depths: a calm and easeful place where the edges of the breath dissolve into limitless space.

Events have been washed out of shape by thinking of them over and over. Sometimes it seems as though none of this really happened and then I come back to the fact of Carl's death.

Thirty One

Carl chased me into the building and up the stairs but I don't know where he is now. I cut my hand on the latch as I rushed into Carl's flat and I am inside with my back against the door, one hand clutching the other hand tightly, covering the cut, staunching the blood.

I keep seeing the moment that I see Molly crouch on the window ledge as the bird flies by and the moment she leaps out and away and falls down. Oh, Molly. I am replaying it over and over on a stuck loop. I hear grunting and scraping and panting. The top of Carl's head appears at the open window.

I experience the violence of extreme fear and it is like being run over, run *through*, by an invisible juggernaut. This horrible lurching feeling of having missed a step stays with me even now.

I am at the window and I slam it shut – I remember doing this – I slam it before I look at him. And then he raises his head and I jump back, away. Carl begins banging his forehead on the windowpane; red face, hair in his eyes and all over the place. Mouth wide open with threads of spittle – delicate, like the start of a new spider's web – connecting his upper and lower teeth.

And the glass breaks, of course. A fairly big piece falls and leaves a volcano-shaped hole in the window, an odd detail but I have it, and other pieces fall, cutting the air down five storeys and shattering on the pavement around Molly's little body. Most of the windowpane is still in the frame. There is more blood now, Carl's. A crunch as shards fall out and maybe a sliver cuts him or a piece gets in his eye because he lets out an animal cry of pain.

He is yelling, demanding entry. I don't think I calculated what would happen if I let him in and then ran out of the flat and down the five flights of stairs. Would I have got away from him? Would he have caught up with me on the cold concrete staircase with the thin echo that nobody would hear? He keeps shouting to be let in, and I open the window.

It happened so fast, and writing it is so slow. The act and the representation of the act, there's a hopelessly wide gap between them.

—

The window doesn't actually touch Carl as I push it upwards but maybe the movement puts him off. Broken glass falls onto our two heads like a handful of anti-confetti. He seems to lose his foothold and he slips down a little but he grabs the windowsill and holds on with both hands. He's frightened now; I can see it in him. He scrambles. I can hear his boots kicking against the wall, desperately searching for anything, anywhere to push up from. He's trying to pull himself up higher, to get an arm over the ledge, trying to pull his head and upper body over the ledge and into the room, to get that balance of weight through the window so he can land with a thud on his own floor, safely. His body is fighting; the organism wants to save itself, but there is a bigger fight going on inside him. I am pretty sure he decides, just then, to let go, because I *see* the decision rise in him, it comes over him like an eclipse.

I reach out. My fingers brush his neck as I take hold of his collar, or what would have been his collar if he were wearing a shirt but he is probably wearing a T-shirt so the fabric in my fist must be a handful of that. I do touch him; touch his skin I mean, touch his bare neck with my hand, but lightly, no more than a brush.

Thirty Two

It wasn't your fault, said my sister.
It wasn't your fault, said the doctors and nurses.
It wasn't your fault, said Shirin and Delilah.

Everybody wanted me to be innocent or to stay innocent and maybe I should have taken this line immediately and stuck to it, singing it like a national anthem in my own country, no questions allowed, unless the questions are patriotic.

Immediately Carl fell, everything became distant. The pills they gave me later made it more distant still. I remember smoking cigarettes and feeling as though I was the smoke. A policewoman gave me the cigarettes and I wondered if she would get them back on expenses.

The police kept asking: Was it your fault? Not in those exact words, but this is what they wanted to find out. A man is dead. Was it your fault? All the questions suddenly became one question and not just *a* question, *the* question: Has a crime been committed?

Thirty Three

When I did speak, it felt awkward – like stumbling, or like I had a sponge for a tongue. I sounded odd to myself but I couldn't work out why and I would ask each visitor: Do I sound weird to you? My sister was the only one who said yes. She said you are falling over your words and they are blurring; it's the pills. It was such a relief to be told this and to realize that the reason I couldn't speak properly was the same reason I couldn't think properly, and it was these massive white tablets they were giving me at regular intervals, the kind of drug that could take down a racehorse, and I did wonder if these pills – so much bigger than the ones I gave myself – were a prize or a punishment.

I have been told that soon after I took my own little pills, I called Johnny and started talking about *getting back to the beach*, telling him urgently that *the glass slipper is on the beach*. He knew instantly that something was terribly wrong, and he called my sister and she called an ambulance and they all rushed to the flat where I was, by now, drowning.

I want to be released from the pressure of this story. I want to deliver the weight of it into the writing and when sometimes I manage it, afterwards I am more relaxed, like a dancer after the dance – limbs tired but hanging effortlessly, body light but grounded, a thing well used.

In a dream I am fighting a big tabby cat, up on its hind legs, the same height as me, and we are engaged in an old-fashioned boxing match. I am wearing boxing gloves but through the padded, balloon-like black gloves, I feel the cat's hard, sharp little teeth against my fist. The fight feels more like a dance because there is no actual violence, though there is a real struggle going on. What stays with me from this dream, even ten years later, is the feel of those hard, sharp teeth through the gloves and a sense of great power – the cat's, not mine – being held back.

I have to be ready to accept bizarre, even frightening things. Stage fright is just too banal to bother with, because if you are vain you don't dare go to those unknown places. All you do is keep yourself safe. You think, Oh that's far enough, that will do, they'll buy this much. And it's not real. Not real at all.

Jeanne Moreau

I knew, somewhere, that what I needed was a sitting down moment. A simple, spacious sitting down moment, a rest on a bench with my face in the sun and let it all come down and meet the floor, landing gently, in its own good time. I knew this but I didn't dare to act on the knowledge. The drink and the cigarettes and the pills had me. Except, of course, they didn't; I had myself. I was afraid. It seemed easier to carry on playing the part, to keep smoking and drinking and not eating properly, to keep slipping below thought, ducking responsibility. Keep wriggling on the hook.

I like my music empty – just one or two instruments, a piano or a cello or a guitar, a voice maybe. I like to enter the music and walk around in it or if I can't achieve that, then I like to get right up alongside, reach into the music and pull out an empty feeling.

In hospital I sometimes thought I could hear a piano being played several rooms away and I would go wandering down long shiny corridors with swing doors, the hospital body's own system of veins and valves, in search of this music that I never found and eventually concluded that it must be the sound of distant water pipes. I felt that I would like to stay in hospital for a very long time. I just couldn't imagine having to get dressed, brush my hair and teeth, wash myself, prepare food; what a lot of time and effort it all seemed to take.

I started to make my own rules. I decided that there are only two emotions, love and fear, and that all the others are shades of these. I made lists:

List 1 – Love
List 2 – Fear

Courage, enthusiasm, kindness are all forms of love. Elegance, respect, forgiveness too. Anything that tightens the heart – hatred, envy, anger, judgement, greed – comes from fear, the fear of losing. (Stephen King says he thinks fear is at the root of most bad writing, I think he's right and I think that fear is at the root of most bad living too.) What are we afraid of losing? The things that make us feel safe and solid, like property, work, money, power, control, but most of all – love.

One day, working on my Love and Fear lists, happily dividing all of human experience into two neat columns, I had a brainwave. Fear isn't the opposite of love; fear is what arises when love isn't there, so maybe, I reasoned, there is only one emotion. There is only love, and the absence of love.

The novelty of being in hospital began to wear off. There were disturbances. The nurses made private telephone calls just outside the ward. I didn't want to hear the results of their fertility test or what time and on what train their mother-in-law was arriving, but it was as though they were in the same room as me. I reached a point where I couldn't stand it for a minute longer. I wanted to get out of there. I was sick of the slowness and the two rows of bodies whimpering through the night.

I am getting married, said Johnny, at my bedside. And suddenly I can't hear anything because the wind is howling in my ears. I tried to look undaunted but I felt my eyes widen and my mouth and chin collapse, just for a millisecond. Of course he noticed; we reveal ourselves in the smallest gestures.

To the other Rachel, I say, a statement not a question.

Yes.

She is not 'the other' now then, is she? She is 'the one'.

Johnny shakes his head as if this stuff doesn't matter, and then he brings my satin shoes out of his backpack and puts them neatly on the end of my bed.

What the . . . ?!

You wanted them, he says, you asked for them.

I do not remember asking for them, but I know that he is referring to the nonsense I garbled to him on the phone: *the glass slipper is on the beach.*

———

In the middle of one hospital night, a cat appeared at the end of my bed. I sat up and looked at the cat, a dark tabby, like the cat in my dream, except this was a normal sized cat and this wasn't a dream. I felt its weight on the mattress as it picked up its paws and padded up the bed towards me. There was no purring or any other noise, in fact the ward was unusually quiet. I could tell by its atmosphere that this was a wild cat. I held very still, willing it to come closer. The cat came within arm's reach and slowly I put out my hand to touch it and it was gone. I didn't fall asleep again afterwards.

Johnny leaves pretty quickly after presenting me with the glass slippers. I have no right to feel abandoned, yet I do, and I can't smoke or drink my way out of this one. Once he's gone, I go out of the ward and into the corridor and look out of the huge window. Three floors below me is the main entrance to the hospital. I look down and I see Johnny leaving the building; I know it's him because of his height and his curly yellow hair bobbing down the stairs. He has a spring in his step, which irritates me. I am holding the beautiful satin shoes, still a bit stunned by his news – he's only known her for six weeks – and by him bringing me these shoes, which seems like a cheap trick now; confuse the confused lady with a pair of shoes after you have just told her that you are getting married to someone else. He hadn't even approved of these shoes, we fought over them, and now he's handing them to me as if they are some sort of consolation prize. Suddenly I am more than irritated, I am incandescent. I hurl one of them out of the window after Johnny. I aim for his head. He doesn't even notice. The glass slipper lands on the steps.

The cat may have been a hallucination, although I prefer to think of it as a visit from some other dimension because the experience was more real than real. Of course the cat made me think of Molly, though this one was a tabby and Molly was black, but thoughts and memories of other things stirred too, like snowdrop bulbs taking root in dark earth, months before the flowering, a very delicate and secret beginning. I am not sure what the purpose of the cat's visit was, other than to remind me of these, as yet unnameable things.

> Believe thou, O my soul,
> Life is a vision shadowy of Truth;
> And vice, and anguish, and the wormy grave,
> Shapes of a dream!
> *Samuel Taylor Coleridge*

I was convinced that the 'Love and Fear' spectrum was my own idea and then, a while later, I saw the exact same thing in a film. I haven't come across my third list anywhere else, though I now know that H. G. Wells did write something similar, obviously before I wrote List 3.

List 3 – Things there are not

There are no deals.
There is no protection.
There is no return.
Nothing can be singled out.

There are no instructions and no rules.
There is no getting away with it,
There is no getting away from it,
There is no getting around it, under it or over.

There are only choices to make.
Or choices to fail to make.

I decide to go and fetch the shoe myself. It's been kicked and trodden on so it's a bit scuffed, but nobody's taken it. I suppose it is an unremarkable object unless you have invested it with meaning.

My fifth favourite drug, if drink, cigarettes, coffee and hard work are not readily available, is a very hot bath. I find they can knock you out quite nicely. So I shuffle along the wide corridor to the institutional bathroom in my poor old satin pyjamas, which are not feeling particularly royal right now, and lock myself in.

Falling for someone who makes you feel special *because* he makes you feel special says nothing about you except that you are needy. It says that you crave this kind of attention, crave the adoration. It shows up your vanity. Maybe, as long as it doesn't reach such extremes, there's nothing inherently wrong with vanity – perhaps it's just another way of coping; a way of making the world smaller. But if you persist, you are fooling yourself. Look around! You are growing old and leaky, it happens to everyone and it doesn't matter, but it's a fact.

I was wrong about everything, even the music – the water pipes that sounded like a piano playing a great way off – because there is no music now, just hot water thundering out of the oversized taps and a gloomy industrial echo. I turn off the taps and watch my toes disappear in the steam. Everything has evaporated. I think it would be better if I disappeared.

This is not a moment you should have in a bath because things are breaking and they need to fall to the ground and smash into a thousand tiny pieces and not be softened or bloated by water. A whole sense of self is shattering. The pieces that are coming away are hard and they need to hit the ground. This is a point of honour. Contact with the ground must be made, smashing and clattering and splintering, total obliteration of what falls.

Thirty Four

Climbing five floors up the front of a building is risky even if you are calm and focused. Carl was angry and upset. If you can have suicide by cop, it stands to reason, surely, that you could have suicide by climbing. Doesn't it?

I know instantly that Carl is dead. I know this even before his body hits the ground.

Slap!

I lean out of the window, looking down. Blood is already beginning to pillow his head, seeping out from under, not like red wine dashing across a table – it spread slower and seemed thicker, more like the syrupy vodka in the clouded bottle in my freezer.

Though my eyes are on his broken body I am not, in any familiar sense, looking at him. I stay like this. I don't know how long. Were people rushing towards him now? Recoiling? Did some scuttle away again? Was it all done in silence? I stay, watching, leaning out of the window. I am trying to deny it. Then this shock: his whole body shot out one great twitch, the last thrash of a landed fish.

Thirty Five

If I owe a debt, then to whom and how shall I pay? Is ten years enough? I want things to be simple. Sometimes they are. But even when they are not, I tend to bulldoze in and reduce things anyway, make them neat and tidy, easier to cope with. This aspect of myself shows in my writing: the mistakes I make in writing, clichés and sentimentality among them, are the mistakes I make in life. I know this, but it is difficult to eradicate all faults, especially when they have grown slowly over years and formed a mental carapace.

Watching the sky this afternoon, I was thinking how years go by like aeroplanes and how you don't have to 'get through' the day, or the night for that matter, because nights and days pass all by themselves. And what passes for love.

I said that Johnny never again asked me what I had had for lunch but he did; he asked me when he came to visit me in hospital. What did you have for lunch today? Hearing it was like looking at an old photograph that stirred up memories of what we once were to each other.

Love remoulds your inner landscape, creates its own chambers within you. You carry it inside like heart and lungs. Perhaps this is where feelings of ownership and belonging come in. I don't fully understand this process but I think it involves an exchange at a very deep level. Maybe it doesn't matter whether it's someone else's cat or someone else's writing, if you love it and it touches you like this, somehow and in some way it becomes yours.

The first time I stayed at Johnny's parents' house, they put us in separate rooms. In the middle of the night I sneaked into his room and we made love, and afterwards Johnny went downstairs and brought back a midnight feast: his father's port and his mother's homemade cake and big fat sandwiches he made himself; delicious, all of it. We finished it all up and Johnny went downstairs to make the same again. We were young then, with huge appetites, and there was a feeling that there was always more.

In a sitting down moment, which could be any given moment or all and doesn't, of course, have to be taken sitting down, sometimes a soft feeling arises. You might be close to tears, wide-eyed and absorbent, zingy, still, or very private. I read something that reminded me of this feeling: 'I am my own home and this is where I belong, and things keep going forward, endlessly.' This is from a story by

Banana Yoshimoto. The story features a lonely young woman who is given an amulet that has healing qualities. Because I read the stories over and over again, the collection itself became a talisman. This book has been in many bags and opened so often that the spine is frayed at each end and the cover has worn soft at the edges, torn a little in places.

I especially remember reading the stories on holiday by the sea. Quite early each morning Delilah and I would leave our hotel; she wanted to get established on the beach in one of her four bikinis, I wanted my two cups of black coffee. Every morning I would stop at the beachfront cafe, sit for an hour or so, drink my coffee, look out over the ocean and read a story.

All I have is my feeling for the story; a feeling about what belongs and what goes where. Writing starts with a feeling. This feeling lives in the ruins at the back of my head, among other wild creatures. I have to coax it out, invite it to show itself. It is necessary to be quiet and open, and to listen as I try to bring it forward. As it comes, it changes. There is something in its mouth. The creature comes almost into view, drops whatever it was carrying and leaps back into the dark.

We are writing this up as an accident, said the police, as if the way they wrote it – the very fact of their writing it that way – changed or determined or set what actually happened, a substitute for certainty.

The police and the hospital decided I should be released. I don't know why these two big institutions acted at the same time – you'd think, maybe, that the police could have decided first and the hospital could have released me later, preferably not on the same day. But that is not how it happened. The judgements arrived at once. You are free to go, they said, and then *they* said: You are free to go.

The flat opposite is finished; the builders are gone. They have done a good job, from what I can see. I should finish too but it is hard to let go. Elegance has to do with holding things lightly, it means stopping at sufficiency; doing no more than is required, *saying* no more than is required.

You are free to go.

Acknowledgements

I am grateful to the following people for helping me find my way in writing this book.

Nancy Rawlinson, who encouraged me right from the start, always had great suggestions on process as well as content, cheered me on through some of the most difficult stages of writing and who, right at the end, spotted something important.

Catherine Janson, who realized I was a writer before I did, who read about thirteen iterations, managing to be enthusiastic each time, and for her faith that I could do it.

Maggie Gee, for her generosity, insight and advice.

Jenny Turner, Anna Wilson and Jane Campbell for many consoling and inspiring conversations about writing, and life.

Tim Gordon and Zoe Pagnamenta for their sparky interest and helpful introductions.

Paul McDermott for taking me seriously, helping me see what it was I was writing about and his precise observations.

Lila Cecil and Joy Parisi for creating Paragraph, a wonderful writers' space in New York where I finished the first draft.

Donald Winchester, for his kindness.

Thomas Ueberhoff for loving the book and saying so.

Paul Baggaley, Emma Bravo, Nicholas Blake, Jonathan Pelham, Kris Doyle, Sandra Taylor for their enthusiasm.

Georgia Garrett, who responded with warmth and sensitivity to the manuscript and to me, who saw what was missing from the first draft and who championed certain aspects when I wasn't brave enough to.

Kate Harvey, who showed such care and close attention, inspired structural changes as well as fine tuning, who nurtured me with lots of time and who ensured safe transition from manuscript to book.

Permissions

The publishers are grateful to the following for permission to reproduce copyright material:

Hart Crane, 'Voyages I' from *Complete Poems of Hart Crane* by Hart Crane, edited by Marc Simon. Copyright 1933, 1958, 1966 by Liveright Publishing Corporation. Copyright © 1986 by Marc Simon. Used by permission of Liveright Publishing Corporation.

Deborah Garrison, 'I Answer Your Question with a Question', from *A Working Girl Can't Win and Other Poems* by Deborah Garrison, copyright © 1998 by Deborah Garrison. Used by permission of Random House, Inc.

William H. Gass, from *In the Heart of the Heart of the Country* by William H. Gass. Reprinted by permission of David R. Godine, Publisher, Inc. Copyright © 1968 by William H. Gass. Reprinted by permission of the author.

Seamus Heaney, *The Spirit Level*, by permission of Faber and Faber Ltd.

Alison Jarvis, from 'Elegy For A Drummer' by Alison Jarvis.

Sarah Kane, '4.48 Psychosis' © Sarah Kane 2000, courtesy of Bloomsbury Publishing Plc.

Medbh McGuckian, from 'Venus and the Rain' (1994) by kind permission of the author and The Gallery Press www.gallerypress.com.

Georgia O'Keeffe, from *Georgia O'Keeffe* – Copyright © 1976 by Georgia O'Keeffe. Published by The Viking Press. All rights reserved.

Sylvia Plath, *The Bell Jar*, by permission of Faber and Faber Ltd.

Stevie Smith, *Novel on Yellow Paper*, by Permission of the Estate of James MacGibbon.

Daniel Stern, *The Suicide Academy*, copyright © 1968 by Daniel Stern. Reprinted by permissions of George Borchardt, Inc. on behalf of the author.

Francesca Woodman, *Notebook 6* and *Journals*, courtesy George and Betty Woodman

Virginia Woolf, *Diary 3: 7*, by permission of the Society of Authors as the Literary Representative of the Estate of Virginia Woolf.